Cecilia

Families of Dorset Book 3

MARTHA KEYES

AUTHOR'S NOTE

In *Cecilia: A Regency Romance,* you will encounter a character named Lady Caroline Lamb. Lady Caroline is a historical figure who lived and was very well known during the Regency Era. Though this book is a work of fiction, elements of it are based on the historical record. If you would like to learn more, please see the note at the end of the book.

DOVER, ENGLAND 1792

Jacques Levesque hoisted a small, wooden chest from the Comte de Montreuil's ship cabin, hearing a slight tinkering inside as he settled it into his arms and began walking it to the wagon.

The chest was heavy for its size, challenging the nine-year old's strength to its capacity. He knew what was inside—or he could guess, at least. Monsieur le Comte had fit every valuable he could inside the privately-chartered ship they had taken from Calais. And now it was Jacques's job to ensure it was all transported to the nearby inn where they would spend the night.

Jacques's eyes shifted around the port, curious and wary of this new land.

England. He had heard of it time and again, but it was nothing like he had imagined—nothing like the glittering descriptions he had gleaned from Monsieur le Comte's friends in the snippets of conversation he had been able to catch around the Comte's estate.

All Jacques could see was distant green hills on one side and, on the other, flat blue ocean as far as the eye could see.

The chaos of departing from the Comte's home in Montreuil had been acute, a culmination of the growing fear inside the household since the storming of the Tuileries and the anticipated collapse of the monarchy.

Jacques was not sad to leave behind life in France, but he was very anxious and unsure of what to expect with Monsieur le Comte in England. Would he drink less heavily? Would he be less cruel? Or would he become even *more* cruel and demanding?

"Jacques," said his father in an urgent voice. The Comte's arm was draped over the shoulder of Jacques's father, his face pale and lethargic. There was unmistakable worry in his father's eyes.

The journey across the Channel had been a rough one—and the Comte had been not only drunk but violently ill. Jacques's own legs still felt wobbly on the sturdy ground of the port.

"Continue loading Monsieur's things into the wagon," his father continued. "He is unwell, and I am going to accompany him to the inn. This man"— he used his head to indicate a French shipman who nodded and slipped a coin into his pocket —"will assist you and drive you to the inn once you have everything."

Jacques nodded and set the chest down in the wagon with a grunt.

His arms ached by the time everything was loaded and the wagon moving across the cobbled street. But aching or not, he would be obliged to help move everything from the wagon to the inn next.

He sighed, but he knew better than to complain. His father had told him sternly that he was to do whatever was asked of him without a word and to keep perfect track of Monsieur's possessions, for it was only under such a condition that the Comte had agreed for Jacques to join them on the voyage.

Jacques hoisted yet another chest into his arms, pressing forward to the carriage with an extra grunt of determination. He was eager to prove that it had not been a mistake to bring him along. He would ensure the safety of Monsieur's belongings.

The Comte would not trust his valuables anywhere but his own room—he had been clear that everything was to stay with him, and his paranoia would surely continue until they arrived in Dorset where he would be among family and could place it all under lock and key. Though they were relatives, apparently the Comte had never met the Broussards, and yet he seemed to trust them. The ways of the aristocracy were strange to Jacques.

The yard of the inn was loud with animals and voices when the carriage bobbed in, and their arrival seemed hardly to be noticed. Jacques searched for the hired coach his father had accompanied Monsieur in and saw it across the yard.

He peeked into the small, wooden chest he had just transported and quickly snapped it shut, the glinting of a ruby ring lingering in his vision. He lifted the chest into his arms and told the French shipman to remain in place until Jacques could receive instruction from his father and the Comte.

He headed toward the inn door, asking one of the innservants in broken English where he could find the French monsieur.

When Jacques arrived upstairs, it was to the sound of imperative voices speaking within the room he had been directed to. Opening the door slowly with his shoulder, he looked inside to see his father and an unfamiliar young gentleman, kneeling beside the prostrate form of the Comte.

The young man rose quickly and turned for the door, his expression urgent and grave.

"No," Jacques's father said in French, his shoulders slumping as he wiped his sweaty brow with a forearm. "It is too late."

The young man stilled and nodded, eyeing the Comte with a frown. "I am sorry," he said in mediocre French. "We did all that we could. My name is Retsford. I am just two rooms down if you need anything."

Jacques's father offered no response, staring at the body in front of him with a stricken look in his eyes.

The man Retsford opened the door, glancing at Jacques with a grimace before pushing past him.

Jacques's father crossed himself and then let himself fall back into a sitting position, with his back against the wall as he ran his hands through his hair.

"Father?" Jacques said hesitantly, setting down the chest.

His father's head came up, and Jacques felt a flash of fear at the sight of his hopeless expression. His father motioned for him to come, and Jacques walked over, shooting a brief, sidelong glance at the motionless body on the floor. Why wasn't Monsieur on the bed where he could sleep comfortably? It would likely be hours before he awoke, if the amount he had drunk aboard the ship was any indication.

"He is dead," his father said, a catch in his voice.

Jacques's eyes widened, and he looked at the form of the Comte, swallowing. There *was* something different about the Comte; something missing.

But dead? Jacques had never seen death up close. Of course, his mother had died giving birth to him, but he didn't remember that at all. His father was his only family.

He felt mesmerized by the sight of the Comte, and yet he was afraid. How did death look so similar to and yet so different from sleeping?

He looked to his father, fear taking an even greater hold at the sight of the dejection there. What would they do now? They didn't know a soul in all of England. Did this mean they would go back to France?

He shivered. What would they do there without Monsieur le Comte to serve? They would be homeless, penniless. They already *were* penniless. The Comte was not a particularly generous master.

Jacques thought of all the jewels and valuables sitting in the wagon, waiting to be brought upstairs to the Comte's room. He thought of the ruby ring he had just seen. Surely the Comte wouldn't be upset if they had to use one small trinket to buy their passage back to Calais? Or a spot on the Diligence—or whatever it might be called in England—to London? One small trinket out of hundreds.

"I saw a ruby ring, Papa," he said in a miserable voice, looking up at his father, whose face was covered by his hands. "Would that be enough to buy passage on the packet?"

His father shook his head in his hands. "It is not ours, Jacques."

Jacques felt a small stirring of hope. "Shall we stay in England, then?"

His father shook his head again, and Jacques fell into a confused silence.

A knock sounded at the door, and Jacques jumped up, moving to open the door a crack. His father didn't stir.

The French shipman stood outside, a question on his face.

"The Monsieur's things," the man said. "Shall I bring them up?"

Jacques looked at his father, who shook his head and then froze, an arrested expression in his eyes.

Jacques waited. "Papa?"

His father blinked twice and looked at Jacques. He nodded at him. "Have him bring them into the next room."

"Yes, please," said Jacques to the servant. "Into the room next door."

The man nodded and left.

Jacques's father stood and began pacing up and down the room next to the body of the Comte. His hand pulled nervously at his lips.

"It could work," he said, stopping and staring at the papered wall. "No one would know." His gaze moved down to the body beside him, and he shook his head again, resuming his distracted pacing of the room.

"Know what?" Jacques said.

His father came over and kneeled in front of Jacques, putting a hand on each shoulder and looking him in the eye with a strange energy Jacques found disturbing.

"It will not be easy, my son," his father said. "But you know how things work in noble households. Can you imagine yourself to be the son of a Comte instead of the son of a valet? Can you act the part of a noble?"

Jacques swallowed and nodded.

His father put a hand on Jacques's cheek. "God has given us an opportunity for a better life, thanks be to Him." He looked toward the window, his jaw tight and hard. "I will not waste it."

2

LONDON, ENGLAND 1813

Cecilia Cosgrove clasped her gloved hands together, stealing a glance at the man and woman approaching the ballroom floor in front of her. Miss Bernard's and Lord Brockway's smiles as they broke arms and took their places in the set were uncomfortably intimate and caring—as if they were unaware that they were surrounded by people, lost in a world of their own.

Cecilia's chin tipped upward.

Their engagement still rankled.

It was not that she begrudged either of them their happiness. But her pride had taken a blow when Lord Brockway's affection and attention had transferred to Miss Bernard, particularly after the warnings from Cecilia's sister Isabel that she would lose Lord Brockway if she wasn't careful.

And she *had* lost him; lost the only man who had seen past her beauty to the other things she had to offer. It had frightened Cecilia at the time and made her uncomfortable—she had never felt so vulnerable or so inadequate. She was accustomed to men admiring her beauty, to flirting with them and piquing their interest while making sure to stay just out of reach—maddeningly so.

But Lord Brockway had wanted more from her—more than her arch smiles and teasing comments. She could see now that she had not taken the right approach. She had tried *harder* to make him jealous when she should have given him an indication that she appreciated his attentions, however little she knew how to respond to them.

She had taken his loyalty for granted, and he had taken it elsewhere.

"A very good pair, those two," said Mary Holledge at her side. She glanced at Cecilia, who hoped that her blush would mask the heat creeping into her cheeks. She knew what Mary thought of the way she had handled things with Lord Brockway. And what was worse, she knew Mary was right.

Mary disliked her—that was no secret—but Cecilia was grateful for her company all the same. Cecilia had hardly ever given a thought to Isabel's constant presence at balls and parties, but she had felt an unexpected loneliness since Isabel's engagement and marriage. It had forced upon her the humiliating realization of how few friends she had.

Cecilia's mother had told her not to mind that only gentlemen seemed to seek her out.

"The other young women are all simply jealous, and for good reason, my love," Mrs. Cosgrove had said. "Who would wish to stand near you and be cast into the shade by your lovely face?"

But Mary, with her candid ways and eagerness to put Cecilia in her place, had quickly put such a notion to rest. "Of course none of the other girls wish to stand near you when you have been so terribly rude and condescending to them."

Mary suddenly straightened with a quick intake of breath, craning her neck to see over the large peacock feather in the matron's cap in front of them. "He came! I have been waiting all season to see if he would come to town," Mary said.

"Who?" Cecilia tore her eyes away from Lord Brockway.

"The Frenchman," Mary said simply. "I have heard of him 'til I am sick to death of his name, but I have never seen him with my own eyes." She looked at Cecilia. "Le Vicomte de Moulinet. You know him, of course."

Cecilia shook her head, then paused. The name was vaguely familiar.

"I thought you might have," said Mary, "for he is a cousin to *your* cousins. The Broussards—on their French side, of course."

Cecilia watched the man entering the ballroom with his blue jacket and gray waistcoat, and her brows drew together. "Oh! I think this must be the Jacques that Letty is forever going on about. I hadn't realized that he was titled."

Or so handsome. She tilted her head to the side. "He doesn't *look* French. Nor does he dress like a Frenchman." She wondered how his eyes looked from a closer distance. Even from two dozen feet away, it was evident that they were a piercing color.

"That is because he has lived in England most of his life, silly. He and his father were émigrés before the turn of the century." Mary sighed. "I doubted the reports I had heard—I have found that people tend to romanticize Frenchmen when they are only just passably good-looking—but I am afraid Lord Moulinet is every bit as handsome as I was given to believe."

Cecilia thought so, too. And a French Viscount, no less. She was intrigued. She had never been courted by a Frenchman.

As if following Cecilia's train of thought, Mary added, "Unfortunately, though, we must all content ourselves with admiring him from afar, as I understand he has no interest in courting."

One of Cecilia's brows went up, and her smile built slowly. No interest in courting? She certainly must see if what Mary said was true.

It would be easy enough to gain an introduction if he was truly related to her cousins, and it seemed that Mary had spoken correctly. Even now, Cecilia saw her mother as well as her Aunt Emily and cousin Letitia Broussard in conversation with Lord Moulinet.

So they had finally agreed to bring Letty to town, had they? The girl would be ecstatic. Cecilia only hoped Letty wouldn't follow her around as she had often done over the years.

Cecilia worked on a mental strategy for how she might be introduced to the Viscount without seeming too forward, and she was given the opportunity sooner than she had anticipated. Lord Moulinet and Letty joined the set forming on the ballroom floor, and Mary was asked soon after, leaving Cecilia to seek out the company of her aunt and mother. Normally, Cecilia would have been embarrassed to be left without a partner, but she was glad in this one instance, knowing that she would certainly meet the French Viscount once the set was over.

"Aunt Emily," Cecilia said as she approached. "What a happy surprise! I had no idea that you would be coming to town, particularly so late in the season."

"Yes, well," Aunt Emily replied as they embraced, "I finally gave in to Letty's pleas, though what came over me, I can't imagine! Giving up Symondsbury and the coast for London in May? But here we are! Ready to enjoy the least pleasant part of the season." She fanned her face, sending a playful wink at Cecilia, who laughed.

"And with a visitor in your midst, no less!" Cecilia looked to Lord Moulinet, who was guiding Letty down the set with a kind expression likely meant to encourage her—she looked terribly uncertain of herself.

Cecilia remembered the terror of dancing her own first set and simultaneously felt a pang of sympathy for Letty and a desire to give Lord Moulinet a partner more capable of doing justice to his own skill.

"Yes," Aunt Emily said with an approving glance at the couple. "My nephew Jacques, you know. The Vicomte de Moulinet, and his father is le Comte de Montreuil, but I am afraid you shan't meet him, for he did not accompany Jacques to town."

"How is it that I have never met either of them?" Cecilia said.

Aunt Emily gave a little shrug. "They dislike London. They

prefer to spend time at their estate in Honiton, but we see them often enough, as it is only a matter of 20 miles from Rothwick Park."

Cecilia laughed incredulously. "What kind of a Frenchman prefers the country to the town?"

Aunt Emily smiled as she watched her daughter and the vicomte. "Jacques is not your average Frenchman, by any means." She clenched her teeth anxiously, and her fan stopped pulsing through the air as she waited for Letty to perform one of the more involved figures of the dance. "Letty has never been at her ease on the ballroom floor, but she is at her best with Jacques because he knows how to calm her nerves."

Cecilia followed her aunt's gaze and watched Lord Moulinet say something which broke through Letty's concentrated state and made her laugh. He exaggerated the next step of the dance, drawing another unsuccessfully-suppressed smile from Letty, and Cecilia found herself smiling as she watched him entertain Letty.

How would she and the vicomte look together on the floor with just such laughs on their lips? They would certainly draw attention. Cecilia drew attention wherever she went.

Lord Moulinet and Letty made their way off of the ballroom floor with wide grins, but as Letty was stopped by a friend who accompanied her to perform an introduction, Lord Moulinet was alone by the time he reached Aunt Emily, Cecilia's mother, and Cecilia.

Cecilia noted her heart picking up speed as he approached. His dark brown hair and eyebrows made his sage-colored eyes stand out as they surveyed Mrs. Cosgrove and then her.

She watched for the familiar pause and subsequent admiration that lit up gentlemen's eyes upon first meeting her. "An angel fallen earthside—" that was how she had been described by one gentleman earlier in the evening.

But she looked for the admiration in vain.

There was no distinction between the way Lord Moulinet's eyes quickly scanned Cecilia's mother and the way they scanned Cecilia herself. If anything, his surveyal of her was so rapid as to be dismissive. The unexpected lack of reaction shook Cecilia's confidence for a moment.

She privately acknowledged the hypocrisy of her thoughts—had she not been lamenting the loss of the one man who had seen past her beauty? Only to now take offense when another man failed to acknowledge it?

"Ah, Jacques," said Aunt Emily, "allow me to introduce you to my sister Mrs. Susan Cosgrove and her daughter Miss Cecilia Cosgrove."

He bowed politely to Cecilia's mother and then to Cecilia, who donned her most engaging smile as she curtsied.

Was there a hint of mockery in his eyes?

"I must tell you, my lord," said Cecilia's mother, "how fortunate it is that you should have the opportunity of making my daughter's acquaintance in this moment, for she is nearly always dancing, with each dance reserved ahead of time, sometimes days in advance. A very successful season she has had!"

Cecilia smiled through fluttering lashes, watching for the vicomte's reaction to the revelation.

"I felicitate you," he said with another small bow, unmoved by the praise.

Cecilia's smile flickered, and she looked down with the pretense of adjusting a glove, trying to ignore the feeling of foolishness which niggled at her. Surely the Vicomte must suspect that her mother's words were simple exaggeration, or else Cecilia would already be engaged for the set forming on the ballroom floor. She felt an annoying need to defend the singular circumstance.

"Mr. Clifford had requested this set earlier in the evening," she said, "but he was obliged to excuse himself on account of falling ill."

Lord Moulinet's eyebrows drew upward as if he had not expected an explanation. "How unfortunate for him. But for you, perhaps it is a welcome opportunity for some rest." He had only the slightest hint of a French accent as he spoke, a peculiarity which added to his attraction.

Having expected him to request to stand in for Mr. Clifford,

Cecilia felt vexation pulse through her. The man seemed determined to pay her only the attention the merest civility required of him.

"Why don't the two of *you* join this set?" Aunt Emily said as the orchestra members strummed their instruments in preparation for the next dance. "There is just enough time."

Lord Moulinet nodded. "Gladly," he said. He offered his arm to Cecilia, and her jaw clenched.

She would have much preferred Lord Moulinet asking her to dance of his own free will rather than complying with a request or fulfilling an obligation.

She stole a glance at him, but his expression was indecipherable. Where was the smiling, laughing lord she had watched with Letty?

At least they wouldn't have the interference of anyone else as they danced the set. They squeezed in at the end of the long line of couples, and Cecilia felt secure in knowing that she would have ample time to change the vicomte's strange inclination to pay her as little heed as he could.

"How are you enjoying London, my lord?" she asked, determined to win over the Frenchman.

"Hardly at all," he said baldly.

She raised her brows and glanced at him. He wore a half-smile, and she felt a buzz of irritation. Who was this Frenchman who thought himself above the *ton?* "Have we made such a terrible impression on you?" she said, trying to keep the irritation from her voice.

"I only mean," he said, "that I have hardly had time to enjoy London. We only arrived last night from Devon."

"Oh."

He glanced at her with a half-smile, and she could only feel grateful that she was spared the necessity of responding as they parted to stand across the set from one another.

Cecilia looked down the line and noted Letty standing across from Mr. Vincent, one of the more accomplished flirts in the room. Letty was far too naive and shy to depress Mr. Vincent's pretensions. She looked as though she was doing her best to fight her nerves, and

Cecilia determined to have a talk with Letty as soon as possible. She needed some guidance on how to go on among vipers like Mr. Vincent.

"I hope," Cecilia said as they awaited their turn, "that London will be to your liking once you have had an opportunity to experience more of it."

"I anticipate that some of it will be, and some of it will not."

"It is true," Cecilia said as they linked arms and moved about the line, "that the company is varied in town. It is somewhat of a maze, in many ways. All the more reason to ensure you allow those with more experience to guide you so that you do not find yourself in the wrong company." She smiled at him.

He raised his brows at her. "What sort of *wrong* company do you anticipate I should find myself in?"

She shot him a significant look. "If you are used to the country, my lord, then you will find it much more difficult to distinguish between the classes in town, for there are many who, at first glance, appear to belong to our class but are in reality of more vulgar birth."

The corner of his mouth pulled up into a half-smile, and his nostrils flared lightly. "What a happy skill you possess to be able to separate the wheat from the chaff with naught but a glance."

She laughed, though she couldn't help wondering if she had offended rather than amused or impressed him. "It requires experience, to be sure, but you will undoubtedly have people to assist you in these matters."

"People such as yourself," he offered.

Was he teasing or sarcastic?

"I believe you could do worse," she said with a provoking smile.

Instead of the responsive grin she expected, he scanned her face, his own expression unreadable.

Feeling the heat rise up her neck and into her cheeks, she tried to maintain her smile. His lack of reaction was as unexpected as it was mortifying.

"Pray, enlighten me, then," said Lord Moulinet, looking around the room. "Who am I to come to know? And who am I to avoid?"

"Well," Cecilia said matter-of-factly, "it all depends upon your goal, for everyone comes to town with a goal in mind"— she leaned in toward him, feeling the familiar thrill of proximity and aware of the way it would affect him —" whether or not they admit it."

He didn't pull away from her, but nor did he lean in closer. So far, he seemed immune to her charms and flirting. She didn't know what to make of the vicomte. "And what is *your* goal, Miss Cosgrove?" he asked.

She blinked twice. There was nothing of dalliance, nothing provocative about his words, as there might have been with any other gentleman. It was a challenge more than anything.

He watched her with interest, though, and she forced a light laugh.

"*That* is neither here nor there," she said, tossing her head lightly.

"Why?" he said, still watching her.

"Because we are talking about *you*, not me." She found it difficult to meet his eyes and instead settled for watching the couple next to them complete the next figure of the dance. She looked further down the set and grimaced as Letty mistook one of the steps, causing an inelegant shuffle on Mr. Vincent's part to avoid trampling her feet.

Cecilia could feel the Viscount's eyes on her.

"It is a shame," he said, turning his head away as they joined arms again and moved down the set.

Cecilia was obliged to wait to inquire as to his meaning until they had taken their places in the line again. Was he speaking of Letty's misstep?

"What is a shame?"

"Your mask," he said, smiling at Letty as she passed by. It was a genuine smile, one he seemed able to call up at will for Letty, and one he had yet to direct toward Cecilia.

She blinked, and he looked at her with one of his brows raised, the same hint of a smile on his lips which she couldn't quite peg as mocking or genuine.

She swallowed, feeling lightheaded at the sight of his frank gaze, which seemed to pierce through her ever-thinning veneer of confidence. With every exchange of words, she felt more flustered and more aware of how utterly out of her control was their interaction.

"I don't think I understand," she said, brushing at a hair on her forehead.

"I know a mask when I see one, Miss Cosgrove," he said with a wry smile. "What I do *not* know is why you wear *yours*." His eyes narrowed as he looked at her searchingly.

Cecilia's mouth opened and closed wordlessly. "You accuse me of affectation?" she finally asked.

"Is it an unjust accusation? We have been dancing for several minutes now, conversing the entire time, and yet I find that you have only conveyed frivolous information about society, while communicating nothing about yourself—or at least not communicating it consciously." His eyes challenged her, and she had the strangest feeling that, whatever persona she had been attempting to portray to Lord Moulinet, he was seeing through it with maddening and frightening facility.

She sucked her cheeks in. "Not consciously communicated?" She needed to know what he meant, and yet she dreaded the answer.

"I mean to say that whatever I *have* come to know of you is *in spite* of what you have said rather than by virtue of it."

She felt her hands sweating inside her gloves and clenched her jaw.

She was used to light flirtation and polite nothings as she danced. This blunt attack—for she knew not how else to characterize it—was new and uncomfortable territory for someone who considered herself somewhat of an expert at making enlivening conversation.

"Pray, enlighten me, then," she said, and the corner of his mouth lifted at her reference to his own words. "What do you know of me already? What have you managed to discover with such ease?" She felt her cheeks burning in mixed anger and embarrassment.

He scanned her face with his horridly intriguing eyes. "I do not wish to cause offense, Miss Cosgrove."

Her eyebrows shot up, and she felt her command over herself slipping. She needed to put this man in his place. "Oh! You believe that to communicate what you have gleaned about me from these two short dances would be to give offense?" She scoffed. "How very flattering you are, *Monsieur de Moulinet*. I had been told that Frenchmen were masters in the art of dalliance, but you have exceeded expectations."

He looked at her with something she could only identify as approbation. "Bravo," he said. "I would rather you insult me in anger than deceive me with empty words and self-importance. You are more than you pretend to be, Miss Cosgrove. Surely what is behind the mask you wear is of more value and more worthy of admiration than the mask itself."

To Cecilia's mortification, she felt her eyes burn. "I did not choose this mask, my lord."

"Perhaps not," he said softly. "But you may choose not to wear it, all the same. What are you so afraid of people seeing?"

The cello strung out its last note, and Lord Moulinet's eyes held hers for a drawn-out moment before he bowed.

3

Jacques threw a backward glance at Miss Cosgrove, whom he had just left with her mother.

He sighed as he walked toward one of the tall sets of French doors which were open to let in a much needed breeze. He stepped out and onto the terrace, which he leaned his elbows on. The garden terrace below, with its tall shrubs and scattered benches, was empty, with only the light from the brightly-lit drawing room windows illuminating it.

Jacques ran a hand through his hair, grateful for the relative solitude but wishing there was something more like the winding lanes and copses of trees around the estate in Honiton.

How would he survive in London if he was already struggling to keep his composure?

He shouldn't have behaved toward Miss Cosgrove as he had. He hardly knew what had come over him. There was something about walking through a room full of wealthy people dressed to the nines, trying to impress one another with their airs—it had grated him all evening, more than he realized.

And then to be introduced to Miss Cosgrove, who seemed to

personify everything he disliked about the town...it had been too much for him to maintain his always-amiable façade.

He, who wished more than anything to be able to dispose of the appearances he was forced to assume, stood in the midst of people who *chose* to deceive one another for no apparent reason.

After years of refusing, he had finally agreed to come to town, with the very small hope that he might find a young woman he could be honest with about his origins; a woman who would love him for the truth that no one else knew.

It had been silly to think that it was a realistic aim—Miss Cosgrove had plainly stated the same prejudice that pervaded the beliefs of those who claimed gentility: no one whose origins were anything but genteel should be countenanced. Had Miss Cosgrove known the truth about Jacques, she would have treated him with contempt and disgust instead of trying to flirt with him.

He closed his eyes and took in a breath. It would be a miracle if he was able to maintain his calm and cheerful manner for the next two months, particularly if he was destined to dance more with young women like Miss Cosgrove, with their affectation, empty smiles, and fluttering eyelids.

He raised himself off of his elbows and squinted into the darkness below as two figures entered the garden.

He had little trouble recognizing the glowing hair of Miss Cosgrove or the timid movements of his cousin Letty—timid only since their arrival in town. The Letty from Rothwick Park was anything but timid.

What were they doing, escaping into the garden alone? He knew Letty practically worshiped Miss Cosgrove. He had heard enough about the young woman to feel confident that he would not like her, even before meeting her tonight—her and her terribly unsubtle mother.

Letty was young for her seventeen years and very impressionable, though, and Miss Cosgrove had a definite hold on her, whether she realized it or not.

Jacques grimaced. He hardly thought Letty would be improved by adopting her cousin's artificiality.

"No," said Miss Cosgrove, taking Letty by the hand, "it is that you have missed one of the steps entirely, and that one missed step throws everything off afterward for the rest of the figure. Come, I will show you. You must pretend that I am a gentleman."

Letty giggled. "But you are much too beautiful to be a gentleman, Cecy."

Cecilia threw her chin high in the air. "Nonsense," she said in a lower voice. Jacques could barely see the smile she suppressed in the dimly lit garden, and he found his own mouth turning up on one side responsively.

"You must learn the steps so that they are instinctive," Miss Cosgrove said as they performed the figures of the dance. "Confidence is key, Letty. One may have everything to recommend one, but without confidence, it is all wasted. And you, my dear, deserve to be as confident as anyone in that ballroom."

"Surely not to be as confident as you," Letty said with awe in her voice.

"Why ever not?"

"Because you are beautiful and accomplished and"— Letty sputtered a moment —"simply everything that all the young women wish to be. I am plain and dull."

Jacques stilled. He hated to hear Letty compare herself, as she so often did, to her cousin and other young women she admired but thought herself below. If Miss Cosgrove did anything to further wound Letty's confidence, he didn't know that he could ever forgive her.

Miss Cosgrove stopped their dancing and put a hand on each of Letty's shoulders. "You are *not* plain and dull, Letty. I don't ever want to hear you say such things again. You are kind and witty." Cecilia touched one of Letty's curls. "And I always wished for dark hair like yours."

"You did?"

Miss Cosgrove nodded.

"But why?" Letty said with a touch of disgust. "Your hair is divine!"

Miss Cosgrove shook her head. "It is just hair, and sometimes I wish to shave it off entirely."

Letty laughter, but Miss Cosgrove pressed on. "My point is simply that none of us is perfectly satisfied with our appearance. Besides, beauty can be its own trial. It does not solve all of one's problems."

"A trial? Surely not!"

Jacques found himself wishing he were near enough to see Miss Cosgrove's expression, to be able to know what was passing through her thoughts in that moment. But he would have to settle for her voice. He knew he should not be listening in to a private conversation, but he found he couldn't tear himself away. The woman he was listening to was nothing like the one he had danced with.

"Yes, Letty. For beauty doesn't endure. And once my beauty is gone, so too will be the admiration."

Jacques found himself leaning farther and farther toward the garden below, straining to hear every word Miss Cosgrove spoke. So, this was what was behind the mask?

"But what use is it to dwell on such a thing?" Miss Cosgrove said. "Your time and energy is much better spent in other endeavors, like learning the steps of a dance well enough that you may enjoy yourself while dancing." She smiled and spun Letty around. "No one can take your confidence or your enjoyment, after all. You must strive to have as much confidence as Princess Caroline, for she is not at all beautiful, and yet people cannot help but like her."

"Except her husband," Letty said significantly.

"Very true." Miss Cosgrove laughed, linking arms with Letty and guiding her back toward the house. "But there is no accounting for the Regent's tastes, is there?"

Jacques smiled and turned back toward the open doors, the touch of guilt he felt for having eavesdropped almost entirely overwhelmed by the appreciation he felt for the scene he had witnessed.

Jacques watched Letty's grand hand gestures with amusement as she recounted her experiences at the ball the night before to her mother, as though she had not observed it all herself.

Where she had entered the ball timid and nervous, she had left smiling and satisfied. Jacques couldn't deny that the shift had occurred after Letty's exchange with Miss Cosgrove in the garden. Jacques had been wary of Miss Cosgrove's influence, but in this instance, there had been a marked improvement in Letty.

"...And I believe that it was fortunate that Jacques was there, for having the Vicomte de Moulinet as my first dancing partner ensured that everyone took me seriously."

Jacques laughed, meeting eyes with his Aunt Emily, who was smiling appreciatively at her daughter.

"I had no idea that my name carried any weight in London," Jacques said, sitting back and sipping his coffee.

"Well," said Letty in the tone of one who was possessed of hitherto-unknown information, "there has been a great deal of mystery surrounding Jacques's identity, I can tell you, for no fewer than five young women inquired after him from me, all wondering how it came to be that they had never before seen such a handsome man—and a French Viscount, no less."

She wagged her eyebrows at Jacques, who merely scoffed. The compliments meant little to him, for he knew them to be shallow and contingent upon everyone's belief that he was truly the Vicomte de Moulinet, heir to the Comté de Montreuil.

"I know," Letty continued, "that everything happening in France has been awful and horrible, but I must admit that I am grateful for the Revolution, if only because it brought us you, Jacques."

Jacques managed a grateful smile. He felt the same way, of

course. The Broussards had been a godsend when he and his father had first arrived at Rothwick Park in Dorset, speaking hardly any English, trying to appear as noble émigrés amongst unfamiliar relatives, when the truth was that they were just two Frenchmen from the *tiers état*—a frightened young boy and his father, determined to make a better life than the one they'd had. The intimate knowledge Jacques's father had of the dead Comte—a result of years of loyal service—had been invaluable in maintaining a persuasive act. And when they had made the inevitable errors, they always had the language barrier and the generous dispositions of the Broussards to fall back on.

"What was it like?" Letty said, her brow furrowing as she reached for the preserves. "During the Revolution, I mean."

"Good heavens, Letty," said Aunt Emily, her eyes flitting to Jacques. "That is hardly a subject for the breakfast table."

Conscience-stricken, Letty apologized to Jacques. "I have just heard so many stories, and it is hard to believe that they are true."

Jacques felt his body tensing. It had been twenty-one years, but he would never forget what it felt like—the oppressive uncertainty of it all, the contagious paranoia of Monsieur le Comte, the constant news of death and change and destruction. "I can hardly confirm the truth of whatever stories you have been told without being acquainted with them. Suffice it to say that we heaved great sighs of relief when we arrived on the shores of England."

"And you never wished to return when it all ended? I think I should miss England terribly if we were obliged to leave."

Jacques wet his lips. These were always the most difficult conversations because they reminded him forcibly of the complete forgery he was perpetrating upon people he had come to love as family. To Letty, it might seem unthinkable that he would wish to stay away from the country of his birth.

But there was nothing for Jacques or his father in France. As émigrés—ones formerly employed by a noble—their return would not have been a welcome one.

He smiled at Letty, pushing the unpleasant thoughts to the back of his mind. "Who could ever wish to leave after spending time with the Broussards?"

Letty's birth, several years after Jacques's arrival in England, had been his first and only experience with a baby. Never having had siblings of his own, he had quickly taken to the idea of himself as an older brother and protector of Letty.

It had been that self-imposed role that had finally convinced him to come to town. Years of questions regarding his intentions to marry had done nothing to prompt him toward seeking a wife—he knew the duplicity it would require would kill him. But upon Aunt Emily's invitation to accompany them to town for the remainder of the season, Jacques had finally taken the time to reconsider his position.

The opportunity to ensure the well-being of the impressionable young Letty, along with the negligible chance that he himself might find a young woman he could trust with his secrets—it had been enough to persuade him to accept his aunt's invitation.

"And what of you, Jacques?" said Aunt Emily, not meeting his eyes as she stirred sugar into her tea. "Were you impressed by any of the young women you met at the ball?"

Jacques's thoughts immediately turned to Miss Cosgrove, a fact which caused his nostrils to flare in vexation. Kind as she may have been to Letty, she had made it abundantly clear that his true identity would not be a welcome revelation.

"I was too busy monitoring the dancing partners of Letty"— he cocked a teasing eyebrow at her —"to pay much attention, I'm afraid. I hope each one of them realizes that it is my approval—not Uncle Matthew's—which will be the more major hurdle they face in obtaining permission to pay their addresses."

Letty laughed but looked at him through narrowed eyes. "I beg you not to scare off all my suitors, Jacques. It would be infamous of you if you did."

Jacques shrugged and sipped his coffee. "Take care who you

encourage, and I shan't be reduced to using intimidation or brute force." He winked at her.

He teased her, but he was far from at ease regarding Letty's time in London. Aunt Emily had become more lax with each child, and Letty was the youngest. She hadn't even remarked Letty's absence when Miss Cosgrove had taken her to the garden. The combination of a susceptible young mind, a sizable dowry, and a sweet disposition was a dangerous one.

Jacques could only hope that Letty would heed his counsel and, failing that, that the counsel she received and the examples she looked to follow merited the attention.

If Miss Cosgrove's instruction in the garden was a true indicator of the counsel *she* would offer Letty, Jacques would have less qualms about Letty looking to her for guidance or spending more time in her company.

He tried his best to ignore his own desire to seek out more of Miss Cosgrove's company himself. *That* could hardly lead anywhere good.

It was only a matter of persuading himself of that fact.

4

Cecilia adjusted the sleeveless spencer she wore over her walking dress before taking her bonnet from her maid Anaïs. She had been impatiently waiting all morning for her assignation in the park with Letty, having left the ball with a promise that she would advise her on a few matters—help her know how to get on better in the *ton* as someone only newly out.

Normally, she would have looked on such an outing with little relish, but she had some hope that she might see Lord Moulinet there.

She had been reflecting almost without ceasing upon her interaction with him at the ball—about his criticism of her, his impatience with the affectation he supposed she adopted.

She had been furious when they had parted ways—at the presumption of him instructing her on...well, anything really. This French, country-dwelling Vicomte.

But it had not taken long for Cecilia to realize that under her anger lay hurt and, if she was quite honest with herself, even a bit of hope.

He had been right, after all—much as she wished not to acknowl-

26

edge it. He had taken her confidence, her never-before-challenged ability to charm any gentleman, her talent for guiding an interaction precisely where she wanted it—leaving a man wanting more when the set was over—and he had smashed it all to oblivion.

If Lord Brockway had been impatient with her flirting and teasing, Lord Moulinet had rejected it out of hand. And when she had lost control of her temper, hurling insults at him, he had incomprehensibly shown the first signs of approbation.

Never had she lost mastery of herself in public or in front of someone she particularly wished to please. And while there was certainly embarrassment at the fact, there was also the memory of the changed light in Lord Moulinet's eyes—the interest her tirade had sparked, followed by the way his eyes held hers at the end of the dance with apology and something like a soft challenge.

She was simultaneously impatient and terrified to see him again.

The muffled sound of the front door bell ringing came to Cecilia's ears. "That will be Letty," she said, leaving her bonnet strings untied and hurrying from the room.

She came up short in the corridor, avoiding a collision with her father who smiled at her and said, "Off to the park, eh?" He raised his brows significantly at her. "A *rendez-vous* with some eligible gentleman, perhaps?"

Cecilia forced a smile. Had her father ever talked to her about something besides her marriage prospects? "Just with Letty."

"Oh," he said, somewhat deterred. But his smile reappeared. "Perhaps you will see Lord Retsford while you're there? I understand he is becoming quite marked in his attentions?"

"Yes," Cecilia said, trying to keep the distaste from her voice.

"I admit," her father said with a shake of the head, "that I was cast down when I heard of Lord Brockway's engagement—for I think he would have been quite the catch—but Lord Retsford!" He smiled at her through mischievously-squinting eyes. "It seems you were right not to accept Brockway after all, for Retsford is a much bigger fish."

Cecilia forced another smile at her father. Had she known that her choice would have been between Lord Brockway and Lord Retsford, she would have been much wiser in her behavior toward the former.

"Take care you don't scare him away, now," her father continued. He pinched her cheek. "You just continue looking beautiful, and I am certain it will only be a matter of time before he is here requesting an audience with me."

He patted the cheek he had pinched and continued down the corridor, humming with a pleased smile.

Cecilia's nostrils flared, and she stood still for a moment—the only movement the over-tight clasping of her hands—until she finally exhaled and walked down the stairs to meet Letty.

Letty was chatty and vivacious as they made the walk from Belport Street to the park. Cecilia found herself having to slow the pace her feet wished to take to their destination.

They had only just entered the park when they caught sight of Lord Retsford, a fact which made Cecilia squeeze her eyes closed in frustration.

In theory, the Marquess of Retsford was exactly the type of peer Cecilia had been intent on marrying: titled, wealthy, and even charming when he wished to be.

But he was also a rake, and much older than the brilliant match Cecilia had been dreaming up over the course of the season. His indiscretions had come to Cecilia's ears long before he had begun paying her attention.

At first, she had been flattered—everyone knew that Lord Retsford was enamored of his current mistress and *very* particular in the young women to whom he condescended to pay heed. But the truth was, she disliked his attentions and his compliments. They were too familiar and yet almost indistinguishable from the things she had heard from dozens of other gentlemen. And the light in his eyes when he said them?

She suppressed a shudder.

"Is that Lord Retsford?" Letty said in an awed tone. "I have never met a marquess!"

"Come," Cecilia said, guiding Letty to turn into the other lane, hopeful that he might not have noticed them.

But it was too late. She heard his footsteps growing louder behind them, followed by his familiar voice greeting her.

She clenched her teeth and then turned toward him with a smile. She had to be wise—it wouldn't do to ostracize the marquess. Little as she relished the thought of marrying him, she had known for some time that it was highly improbable that she would be able to marry someone she loved—if she was even capable of the emotion at all.

Her parents had long expected her to put her beauty to the best advantage possible.

"What a wonderful surprise, Miss Cosgrove," Lord Retsford said with his wide, charming smile. His hair was brown, but gray hair peppered his sideburns. His eyes moved to Letty, and one of his brows quirked up.

Cecilia grimaced. Introducing Letty to someone with Lord Retsford's reputation was *not* something she took any pleasure in. It was precisely to warn Letty *against* figures such as the marquess that she had agreed to walk with her in the park.

But Letty was wearing the shy smile that made her look both young and alluring, and the marquess's responsive half-smile needed little interpretation. He was determined to meet her.

He looked to Cecilia to perform the introduction, and she smiled through clenched teeth, wishing she could decline the service without offending him.

"Lord Retsford," she said, trying to keep a bright tone, "allow me to introduce you to my cousin, Miss Letitia Broussard. She is only recently arrived in town."

He put out a hand, and Letty placed her hand in his with a shy, lashed smile as Lord Retsford placed a soft kiss on it.

Cecilia suppressed her irritation at the bold gesture. It was a terrible combination: Letty's naïveté with Lord Retsford's wide experience and calculated charm.

He walked with them for a few minutes, addressing himself primarily to Letty. Cecilia was torn between various emotions: relief that *she* was not obliged to talk with him, a slight feeling of pique that he was almost ignoring her, and dismay that he seemed to have latched onto Letty as some kind of target—whether for harmless, light flirtation or something less benign, Cecilia didn't know.

Based on her shy smiles and the healthy blush in her cheeks, Letty was enjoying her conversation with the marquess, and Cecilia was keenly aware of how he brought the conversation to an end before Letty seemed ready.

Cecilia knew the tactic well, as it was one she had often employed, but it exasperated her to see it employed on Letty.

As they slowed to bid Lord Retsford good day, Cecilia's eyes lighted upon the only sight less welcome than that of Lord Retsford: Lord Moulinet. Her heart fluttered and dropped simultaneously at his appearance, watching him stride toward them with his lips pressed together and brows knit.

Being new to town, Lord Moulinet was unlikely to be familiar with Lord Retsford, but Cecilia couldn't help but feel he would be displeased with the new association if he *had* been familiar with the man.

"We wish you a very pleasant afternoon, my lord," Cecilia said hurriedly, hoping to speed the marquess's departure.

Lord Retsford bowed to them and walked off in his confident gait in the direction of Lord Moulinet.

"Jacques!" Letty said as her eyes fell upon her cousin. "How fashionable of you to be here."

He smiled humorlessly, his hard eyes flitting toward Cecilia. "And of you," he said to Letty. He shot a backward glance at the retreating figure of Lord Retsford. "And meeting all the rakes in town, I see. How kind of your cousin to introduce you."

Cecilia bit her lip. So, he *did* know the marquess's reputation. She found herself wishing she could explain how it had come about.

"How unkind of you, Jacques!" said Letty in agitation. "He is no rake! Lord Retsford was very kind and attentive."

"I am sure he was," Lord Moulinet said dryly. "That is what I was afraid of. You mustn't entertain the attentions of men like Lord Retsford, Letty, however kind and attentive they may be." His voice was stern and unyielding.

"Well, if that isn't outside of enough," Letty said in a sullen voice. "I don't know why you should have taken the marquess in such dislike, but if Cecilia is friends with him, then he must be perfectly respectable, of course."

Lord Moulinet's gaze shifted to Cecilia, and heat crept up her neck and cheeks. She felt her chin lift, almost without her permission.

"Whatever Miss Cosgrove's opinion of Lord Retsford"— his eyes lingered on Cecilia before moving back to his cousin —"I beg you will not encourage his attentions, Letty."

Letty gave only a non-committal "hmph" before saying, "You are determined to be disobliging today, aren't you? I suppose you mean to refuse to accompany Mama and me to the Cosgroves for dinner tomorrow as well?"

Lord Moulinet opened his mouth and then closed it again.

Cecilia didn't know whether she hoped that he would confirm or contradict Letty's words. So far, her experience with Lord Moulinet left her feeling deficient. And, even more frustrating, she found herself wishing to rectify whatever had led him to view her in such a negative light, while her pride demanded she teach him a lesson.

Somehow, though, she doubted whether she was capable of carrying out such a plan.

the vicomte walked with them down the lane, and the ill-temper he had harbored upon meeting them dissipated as they conversed, providing Cecilia ample opportunity to observe the gentler and more amusing manners which had been absent during their interaction the night before.

How could such an amiable gentleman have no intention of marrying? Pleasing manners, a sense of humor, undeniably handsome, wealth, and a title. What was there not to like?

When they parted, Cecilia found herself trying to stifle the hope that he would indeed be present for dinner the next day.

"I am sorry, Cecy," said Letty, after Lord Moulinet had left them. "He is not usually so unamiable, but he obviously has taken Lord Retsford in dislike for some reason."

Cecilia swallowed and stared at the dirt path below. "You know, Letty, there is something to be said for his opinion of the marquess. You remember my telling you to be cautious of associating too freely with libertines?"

Letty nodded, her eyes alert and watchful.

"Lord Retsford is very practiced in the art of making himself agreeable, Letty. But the truth is that he simply knows how to please when he wishes to. He has had years to discover how to make young women like you and me feel as though we are special and unique."

"Oh," Letty said, disheartened. Her forehead wrinkled. "But your mother said that *you* are seen in his company frequently of late."

How could she explain it all to Letty? "It is true, but I have much more experience than you in keeping gentlemen at arm's length. My heart is quite hardened to men like Lord Retsford, you know."

She had thought her heart hardened to *all* men, in fact. And it was for that reason alone that she had looked upon the prospect of marriage to someone like Lord Retsford with any degree of equanimity, for, though her heart would remain untouched, at least she would have position and wealth to ensure a comfortable life.

The stirrings Lord Moulinet had produced in her heart were minor—and confusing—but unexpected enough to make her second-guess her goal of achieving the most brilliant match possible. The irony was not lost upon her that the first gentleman to rattle her desire for the highest peer she could acquire was one who seemed to want her not at all.

If the vicomte *did* attend dinner, perhaps Cecilia would have the opportunity to realize that her sudden hesitation had been as silly as it seemed, and she could put such irrational thoughts back where they belonged. She needed a reminder of why she had been so thrilled upon learning that the marquess had taken an interest in her, of why emotion need have nothing to do with marriage.

ⓢ 5 ⓢ

Jacques dusted the toe of his boot, watching the way the light from the window gleamed off the Hessians.

He hoped he wouldn't regret agreeing to dine with his aunt and cousin at the Cosgroves. He had never met Mr. Cosgrove, but he had heard enough about him to guess that he wouldn't take to the man. But while Jacques was unlikely to find *him* agreeable, Mr. Cosgrove was reportedly always anxious to get on good terms with any nobleman, French or otherwise.

Jacques had often felt sick inside when he attended such gatherings, knowing that he was being welcomed into an abode where his presence would never be countenanced, were the truth known.

But with toadying people like he understood Mr. Cosgrove to be, he often found it amusing instead. His amusement at the prospect, however, was quickly dampened by the thought of Miss Cosgrove— the person he had so recently chastised for inauthenticity.

The disappointment Jacques had felt upon seeing Letty and Miss Cosgrove in the company of the Marquess of Retsford had been unaccountably acute.

That he was afraid of Letty's susceptibility to the man, there was no doubt. Jacques could too easily imagine Lord Retsford's attentions bringing about recklessness and impropriety on Letty's part if she were to succumb to his charm or become infatuated with him, as Jacques had already heard of so many other young women doing.

To add to the misgiving he felt, he had been angry to see Miss Cosgrove as the party responsible for introducing Letty to the marquess. Did she think she was doing her cousin a favor by exposing her to such a man?

Jacques shook his head and sighed as he left his bedroom. He had hoped better of Miss Cosgrove after witnessing her guidance to Letty the night before.

But underneath those two emotions, he had known a sliver of jealousy. Aunt Emily had mentioned that the marquess was growing more persistent in his attentions to Miss Cosgrove, so to see evidence of the intimacy so soon had been discouraging. The two glimpses she had given him—albeit, one unknowingly—of what lay underneath the surface had piqued Jacques's interest and intrigued him. It was absurd, of course, but he found himself curious to see more of Miss Cosgrove.

He handed Aunt Emily and Letty into the coach, hopping in deftly behind.

"I am so glad you decided to come, Jacques," said Letty, adjusting the silver comb in her hair.

"Indeed," Aunt Emily said, "you are always a wonderful addition to any party, my dear."

"It is true," Letty confirmed. "Mrs. Wheeler says that you have the most obliging manners of any gentleman she has met, and the type of breeding that can only be born, not learned."

Jacques stifled a laugh. For some time, his father had been concerned that people would be able to sniff out their low origins, but Jacques had found the *beau monde* to be as inaccurate as they were confident in their assumptions about such things.

"So, you have forgiven me, then?" he said with a teasing wink at Letty.

She smiled widely at him. "Of course I have. I could never stay angry with you. And besides, you were right."

He raised his brows. "I was?"

She nodded. "Yes, for Cecilia told me herself that Lord Retsford is not the type of gentleman whose attentions I should encourage."

Jacques felt his pulse quicken. So, she had lent her support to him, had she? But then why would she herself encourage the marquess's attentions?

"Lord Retsford?" Aunt Emily said with curiosity. "Has he shown an interest in you? I admit that his reputation gives one pause, but—a marquess!"

Jacques grimaced.

"I admit," Letty said, "that I was quite taken with him at first, for he made me feel as though I was someone quite out of the ordinary, but I see now that he is simply an expert at gallantry."

Jacques and Aunt Emily met eyes, unalloyed relief in hers and amusement in his.

When he saw Miss Cosgrove in the drawing room, his impulse was to go to her immediately. Apart from his aunt and cousin, she was the only person in the room he knew, after all. But he suppressed the desire and instead waited patiently for his aunt to introduce him to Mr. Cosgrove, whom he found to be garrulous and irritating.

Miss Cosgrove stood across the room, speaking with a gentleman, but when her eyes met Jacques's, her eyelids fluttered, and she smiled hesitantly at him.

His eyes warmed responsively—he would take the uncertain smile a thousand times over her arch looks.

He felt his arm taken hold of firmly. "Come, my lord," said Mr. Cosgrove gaily. "I must introduce you to my daughter."

Jacques found himself face to face with Miss Cosgrove, the man next to her tossing off whatever was in his glass.

"Allow me to present to you my fair daughter Cecilia. I give you fair warning though, Moulinet, that with such a face and figure as she

36

possesses, there are gentlemen and lords fairly lined up to pay their addresses to her."

Jacques drew back in surprise and watched as Miss Cosgrove's face flushed and she averted her eyes.

The gentleman standing next to Miss Cosgrove looked at Mr. Cosgrove with disgust. He was certainly a brother to Miss Cosgrove—at such proximity, Jacques had no trouble seeing the resemblance.

"Forgive me," said Miss Cosgrove, her voice high-pitched, and her chin raised. "I have a touch of the headache." She executed a swift curtsy to Jacques and then turned on her heel, leaving the room in a dash of white muslin.

Her brother watched her departure with a grimace and then turned to his father. "She's your daughter," he said with a wrinkled nose and black brow, "not a bit of horseflesh to be sold to the highest bidder." He set down his glass with a clank on the nearby sideboard table and walked off.

Jacques stared after Miss Cosgrove, aware that Mr. Cosgrove was frowning next to him.

Mr. Cosgrove shrugged his shoulders and shook his head. "I appear to have very touchy children, Moulinet. Don't regard them," he said, clapping a hand on Jacques's shoulder. "I certainly don't."

Jacques resisted the impulse to withdraw from the gesture. He found the man repellent.

Mr. Cosgrove looked around the room. "Still waiting on Broussard, are we?"

Jacques nodded. "I believe my uncle was coming here straight from White's, sir. I imagine he will be here shortly, but, if you will excuse me, I will go inquire of my aunt." He gave a shallow bow and walked away.

Everyone in the room was engaged in conversation, so he touched Letty on the shoulder, told her he was going out for a breath of fresh air, and left the room.

He rubbed the back of his neck as he closed the door behind him softly and stepped into the corridor, with he knew not what destination. He found himself often needing such respites at social gatherings. People like Mr. Cosgrove were one of the primary reasons Jacques's own position was difficult. The man's words had ignited his temper—one which seemed to be unusually sensitive of late—and reminded him of everything he disliked about the set of people he was obliged to live his life among.

Of course, he didn't wish to return to the life he had led before coming to England, but he had tired of the charade he was required to assume—and the charades of everyone around him, who seemed intent on parading around town day after day and night after night with never a glimpse of what kind of people they truly were. They spoke incessantly of one another in whispering tones, ensuring there was never a chance to speak on any meaningful topic.

But what he had seen of Miss Cosgrove had given him hope. For her, at least.

But people like Mr. Cosgrove made him wonder if the majority of the *ton* wasn't perhaps every bit as superficial and empty as it seemed.

The sound of footsteps ascending toward him on the nearby staircase met his ears, and he slipped through the partially-open door on his left. He wasn't doing anything wrong, being in the corridor, and yet he still felt the impulse to hide.

He looked around the room he had entered—a salon decorated in green—and froze.

Miss Cosgrove sat on one of the chairs near the window, staring at him with wide alert eyes, which she hurriedly wiped free of the tears trickling down her cheeks.

"Oh," Jacques said, blinking quickly. "I apologize—I didn't know you were in here."

She rose from her seat and shook her head quickly. "I shall leave."

Jacques grimaced. "Miss Cosgrove," he said, and she stopped just in front of him, squeezing her eyes shut.

"Please, don't," she said. "Don't say anything. I can already guess what you think of my father. And me."

Jacques frowned. "I imagine that your guess of what I think of you would be very wrong." He exhaled sharply. "I only wanted to thank you."

She looked up at him, a glint of surprise in her eyes. "Thank me?"

He nodded slowly. "For warning Letty against Lord Retsford." He smiled wryly. "Your opinion seems to hold much more sway than mine. Whatever you said, it convinced her completely of his unsuitability." He met her eyes, noticing how a tear still clung to her dark lashes. He suppressed the impulse to dry it. "So thank you."

She swallowed, frowning. "It was the least I could do. When he came upon us in the park, I tried to look for a way to avoid giving an introduction, but it was useless."

"I understand. Men like Lord Retsford know just how to obtain what they wish for." He watched her carefully.

Why—if his aunt's stories were correct—would she encourage someone like the marquess, of whom she didn't seem to approve, in his attentions toward her? Was his wealth and title so alluring as to cancel out all his flaws?

Jacques would be disappointed if that was the case, even though he knew that those were the two main concerns of the society he operated in.

"I hope you mean to join us for dinner," he said with a half-smile. "If you leave me to entertain and respond to Letty's constant dialogue alone, I shall never forgive you."

Miss Cosgrove's smile broke through her furrowed brow, and she looked up at him hesitantly, the smile fading as quickly as it had appeared. "My father..." she shook her head.

"I won't pay him any heed." He paused a moment, but his boldness won out. "And you shouldn't either. Come. I shan't let you escape this evening's entertainment when your presence was the only reason I accepted the invitation in the first place." He sent her a teasing smile, feeling unaccountable lightness fill his chest as he watched her laugh softly and follow him.

❧ 6 ❧

Cecilia sat down at the dinner table, her chin up and her shoulders down. She didn't wish her father to know how his words had affected her—and she didn't know why they had suddenly done so. She was accustomed to the way he spoke.

Lord Moulinet sat down on one side of her, and she shifted in her chair. Did he pity her now? Did he feel he somehow had to protect her?

It would almost be more unbearable than knowing he held her in contempt.

She caught eyes with her brother Tobias, who nodded at her with a thoughtful expression.

Tobias's personality and her own had never agreed—perhaps because they were too similar in many ways. He had always been fonder of Isabel and, on those rare occasions when he decided to come home for a visit between escapades with his friends, he had inevitably taken Izzy's side in whatever tiffs and debates came about.

When he had returned home upon Isabel's engagement, though, his attitude toward Cecilia had been less dismissive than usual.

Whether *she* had changed or he had, Cecilia simply found herself grateful that they were less at loggerheads than in the past.

"Tell me," said Lord Moulinet, taking some soup from in front of him, "is that your brother?"

Cecilia followed his gaze and nodded. "Tobias. He is the eldest."

The vicomte looked at Tobias and then back to his soup. "I like him."

"I am sure he would be flattered, except that you have not had any chance to interact with him to form such an opinion, have you?"

He made a non-committal noise. "Extended personal interaction is not always necessary to form an opinion of someone's character, is it?"

"For you, perhaps not," she said, smiling over at him. "You seemed to form your opinion of me very quickly indeed."

He chuckled. "Formed and then revised."

"Why?" she said, her hands pausing before her.

His mouth twisted to the side, and he shrugged. "I formed my opinion based on what you chose to reveal to me of your character."

"And then?" She cut a piece of the green goose on her plate, ignoring her nerves as she awaited his answer.

"And then revised it when I realized that your character was not what it had at first appeared to be."

Her hands stopped, and she stared down at her plate. "And what if what you first saw *is* part of my character? Not a deception but one of many facets?" She looked at him, and his brow furrowed as he searched her eyes.

"Then you do yourself and everyone a disservice by holding back the most engaging and beautiful facets of your character in favor of the facet you've been told is most important."

She swallowed, maintaining eye contact with him, trying to decide whether to take his words as a compliment or an insult. He spoke plainly with her, and she found that she both appreciated and resented it. It was nothing like the roundabout, strategic dalliance she had engaged in with any number of men since her début.

She never knew quite what to expect from the vicomte.

"And what of you?" she said. "You have never yielded to a desire to please or to conform to what society expects of you?"

He met her eyes with his penetrating gaze, saying nothing as his eyes dropped back down to his utensils. "I have done it often enough that I know how little lasting joy it holds."

"Joy," said Cecilia slowly. "Yes, perhaps no lasting joy. But what of wealth and position and the freedom *they* bring?"

His hands slowed cutting the veal in front of him, and his mouth drew into a thin line. Looking at her with those piercing eyes that quickened her pulse, he said, "One is hardly free if one is obliged to maintain a façade. I begin to think that price too high. To be loved and accepted for one's true self seems to me the greatest privilege in existence."

She scanned his face, wanting to ask him what he meant, why he looked so grave. He seemed to speak from experience, but she could find no trace of guile or deception in him—so where did he draw his wisdom from?

Her chin came down, and she stared at the champagne in her glass, with its scattering bubbles. "And what if to show one's true self would mean not acceptance and love, but disappointment?"

He shook his head. "No one knows such a feeling better than I. But I assure you that such a fate would not be yours, Miss Cosgrove."

She wanted to believe him. After all, she had already shown more real emotion to him than to any other gentleman of her acquaintance, and somehow he seemed not to have developed a distaste for her company; indeed, he seemed to appreciate her for it all the more.

But he was not like most gentlemen she knew.

When dinner had concluded, Cecilia and Letty walked to the drawing room in the company of Cecilia's mother and her Aunt Emily, leaving behind Lord Moulinet, Mr. Cosgrove, Tobias, and Mr. Broussard.

Letty immediately took Cecilia's arm in hers. "Tobias has become quite handsome, hasn't he?"

Cecilia frowned and glanced over her shoulder at the sight of the four men around the table, her eyes finding her brother. "Has he?"

Letty looked at her with incredulity. "Decidedly he is! Even when he was looking daggers at your father earlier, he looked very handsome indeed. I think that he may even be more handsome than Jacques."

Cecilia hid her dubious expression. She was fairly certain that Jacques was the most handsome man she knew. She thought him even more handsome now than she had upon first meeting him.

Letty chatted almost without ceasing, asking Cecilia her opinion on this man and that and whether or not she was of the opinion that so-and-so and such a young lady would make a match of it, to the point that Cecilia began to feel out of patience with her cousin.

After the meaningful conversation she'd had with Lord Moulinet, the gossip seemed empty. She wished she could continue her conversation with him rather than dwelling on foolish nothings.

Thus it was with some small relief, followed by a bout of nerves, that Cecilia watched her mother's approach and listened to her request for a moment of privacy with Cecilia. She found that conversation with her parents had become a source of stress recently, as it so often involved discussion of Cecilia's prospects with the marquess.

They walked toward the pianoforte, leaving Letty and Aunt Emily behind them with the tea.

"My dear," said her mother with a frown, glancing at Cecilia's dress, "I do not think that the pale yellow was a wise choice for you this evening. It makes you look sadly pulled and tired."

Cecilia glanced down at her dress and swallowed. Was her mother right?

She felt a twinge of embarrassment. She had always been complimented when she wore yellow—it was said to bring out the sheen in her hair. Perhaps the dress wasn't the problem. Perhaps her beauty was declining?

"Ah well," her mother said with a breath, "that ship has sailed, I'm afraid. At least we may content ourselves that the marquess was not here." Her mother scanned her again critically, making a clicking noise with her tongue and shaking her head. "Yes, not at all flattering. Perhaps it is best to tell Anaïs to dispose of it so that there is no chance of him seeing you in it."

Cecilia opened her mouth, but she found that she could find no words to respond. Her cheeks began to prick with heat. Her mother was disappointed.

"Speaking of the marquess, my dear, I think you must have a little more care if you mean not to drive him off." She grimaced at Cecilia. "You seem to be on very good terms with the Vicomte de Moulinet, and I am sure he is quite unexceptionable and agreeable, but"— she squeezed Cecilia's arm and drew toward her to whisper— "he is hardly a Marquess."

Cecilia felt her muscles tensing.

"You are charming and beautiful, my dear," her mother continued, "and it pleases me greatly to see your success. You can hardly aim too high, it seems."

The door opened to admit the men, and her mother patted her arm. "What a treat to enjoy a chat with you. Now I must go and see to the guests. I know that I may trust your judgment completely." She smiled at Cecilia and pulled her arm away, moving with her characteristic confidence to the other side of the room.

Cecilia stood motionless for a moment. She had sought her mother's praise all her life, and she had frequently received it.

But never had it felt so shallow. Never had Cecilia considered that praise could actually cause pain as it did now.

Had her mother ever applauded her for anything but her appearance, her ability to attract and captivate those who would add to the family's prestige? Was she so intent upon utilizing Cecilia's beauty that she cared nothing for what would make her daughter happy?

She swallowed. She had always pitied Isabel for her plainness, but for once, Cecilia felt the stirrings of envy.

Isabel's marriage had been regarded as an unlooked-for stroke of good fortune—a boon to be rejoiced over because it added to the brilliant match Cecilia was expected to make. Isabel's plainness might have made life at home difficult, but in the end, it had allowed her to marry for love.

That Cecilia would marry the wealthiest, highest-ranking peer she could attract was taken for granted. Never had anyone considered that she might wish to do otherwise. And for a long time, Cecilia herself had never considered it.

But she was now.

She looked to Lord Moulinet, laughing with Tobias across the room. She couldn't resist a smile when she saw his.

But her own wavered.

What would her mother and father say if she refused to marry the marquess? There was no doubt in her mind that they would exercise every power of persuasion to forbid such an incomprehensible decision.

And truth be told, it seemed fantastic even to Cecilia that she would contemplate foregoing a future as a marchioness when it was within her reach.

7

The arrival of Jacques's father to town was entirely unexpected.

"I thought I would come see how you're getting along, *mon fils*," he said, smiling at Jacques and squeezing his shoulder as he walked up the steps to the Broussard's townhouse. His hair was powdered, as always, and his clothing—with his buckled shoes and green striped coat—was impeccable, despite being a score of years behind the current fashions.

Jacques was glad for his father's company—it always made him feel less alone, less like a solitary impostor.

But his father seemed to harbor none of the qualms that niggled at Jacques more and more each day in town. Perhaps his father's placid confidence was only a façade, though? Jacques had to ask. Surely he couldn't be the only one whose conscience pricked at him.

Mr. Broussard was taking his dinner at White's, so Jacques and his father were left to their port alone after dinner the evening of his arrival.

"What news do you bring from home?" Jacques asked.

His father made a grunting noise as he finished swallowing.

"Nothing happy, I'm afraid. Adam Hewitt's hopes are dashed to pieces, you know."

Jacques set his wrists on the edge of the table. Adam was his closest friend back home. Adam had known himself to be in line for his uncle, Lord Guildforth's, barony for years.

"Dashed to pieces how?"

His father shrugged, pouring more port into his glass. "Guildforth has remarried."

Jacques looked at his father incredulously, covering his mouth with a hand.

"And quite a young, healthy woman at that. I'm afraid there is little chance of young Hewitt inheriting anymore."

Jacques's arm dropped to his side.

Poor Adam. Of course, he had only ever been the heir presumptive, but no one had expected Guildforth to remarry—not at his age, and not with the deep affection in which he had held his late wife. To have every expectation of leading a life of wealth and status, only to have it taken unexpectedly...

Well, it was the exact opposite of what had happened to Jacques. Jacques had done nothing to merit his good fortune, and Adam had done nothing to merit his bad fortune.

Jacques sat back in his chair, his brows drawn together and his jaw shifting from side to side. Had *his* own good fortune been at the expense of someone else's?

"Father," he said, staring at the crimson liquid in the glass in front of him. "Had Monsieur le Comte any family to inherit *his* title?" It was a question which had plagued Jacques at the back of his mind for years. He looked up at his father, whose eyes narrowed. "Have we stolen the life someone else should have had at the Comte's death? A life meant for his heir?"

His father's eyes widened, and he shushed Jacques, glancing at the doors as if someone might be listening. "Keep your voice down, Jacques."

"Have we, though?" He needed an answer. Was someone walking

around the streets of France, destitute because he and his father had capitalized on the opportunity presented them twenty years ago?

His father shook his head. "Le Comte was a singular man, with no family to speak of—at least I never heard him do so."

Jacques rubbed at his cheek thoughtfully. No family at all? It seemed incredible. "You are sure?" He closed his eyes and took in a breath. "I can't rid my mind of the image of some poor wretch whose rightful place we have usurped."

His father scoffed. "Rightful place! By virtue of sharing a blood-line?" His father waved an impatient hand.

"You sound like a Jacobin, Father, a revolutionary. But you and I are reaping the benefits of *l'ancien régime* and all the benefits of high birth."

His father shook his head, staring at Jacques with hard eyes. "We took a small fortune and made it into what we now have. *We* did that."

Jacques nodded thoughtfully. His father was right—it was their careful managing of the Comte's wealth which had allowed them to buy their estate and turn it into one that was healthy and thriving.

"But we could not have done it *without* that small fortune. Or without the title that opened so many doors for us—a title and fortune which were not rightfully ours."

His father made an impatient noise. "Did you think we should have sent the Comte's valuables back to France on the packet? Hoping that they would find themselves in the hands of an heir, if such an heir exists, which I am certain he does not? You would think he would have made some attempt to know the Comte and his lands if he was truly the heir."

Jacques said nothing. He couldn't deny his father's sensible argu-ments. What could they have done with the Comte dead and all his possessions in their charge? The French government would have gladly accepted the treasure, no doubt, and made use of it in furthering its success in the war. But that hardly seemed a preferable outcome to the good Jacques and his father had been able to do.

"Perhaps it is the Broussards who should have received the valuables," Jacques said softly.

His father shook his head for the tenth time. "Their relation to the
Comte is through marriage only—a distant cousin on the Comte's
mother's side." His father sighed, his energy suddenly sapped. "This is
all absurd talk, Jacques. Nothing of le Comté de Montreuil remains
to be inherited, after all that happened during the Revolution. If the
Comte had stayed in France, he would have lost everything he had.
How he knew which way the wind was blowing, I don't know. But he
understood something that the other nobles did not, and we are left to
thank God for that fact and for the opportunity He provided us."

Jacques clasped his hands together, twiddling his thumbs. "You
are right, Father. Of course you are. And yet I find myself wishing
that we weren't obliged to deceive everyone we care about. It is a
heavy burden at times."

"Heavier than the rejection we should face if it were known? You
must not think, *mon fils,* that we are the only ones with secrets. *Le
beau-monde* is full of secrets and scandals that could be the undoing
of their keepers if they were known. Le Comte had secrets of his own
—vile, terrible things which do not bear repeating. He was not a good
man. Have you considered that perhaps God wished for a good man
to take his place? And you, Jacques, are a *good* man."

Jacques tried to offer a smile but knew it was more like a grimace.

His father watched him for a moment, then leaned toward the
table, placing his hands on the edge. "*Écoute-moi bien, mon fils.* Many
of our friends and acquaintances are every bit as indebted to luck for
their good fortune as we are. They are only much less aware and
much less grateful than we. *En plus,* you have been le Vicomte de
Moulinet longer than some of these English peers have held their
titles. There is no logic to it. But at least we may do justice to our
humble origins by using the influence we now have to benefit those
with less good fortune than we."

Jacques nodded slowly.

Surely there was nothing wrong with doing what his father was saying? To reveal the truth about themselves would be to forfeit everything they had worked for and all the good they could yet do. And to what end?

It would bring shame to the Broussards and would benefit no one. No.

Surely the past was best left where it was: forgotten by everyone else and, with any mercy, forgotten by Jacques himself in time.

8

The line of carriages outside the Simmons' townhouse stretched down the street and wrapped around the corner, while the hustle and bustle of passing equipages continued in the congested lane.

"I don't see why we have to leave so early," Letty complained as she stepped into the Broussard's coach, "when we shall undoubtedly be obliged to sit in the carriage for three quarters of an hour waiting for our turn to leave."

Jacques shot an amused glance at Miss Cosgrove. Quite opposite from Letty, Jacques found himself feeling grateful that his aunt had asked to leave the ball at an earlier hour than was her custom. He was content to rest in the carriage in the company of Letty, Miss Cosgrove, and Aunt Emily rather than to continue dancing and talking in the overheated ballroom.

"You are directing your complaints to entirely the wrong person," he said as he handed Cecilia in with a smile. "Your mother was the one who insisted upon leaving right away."

"Yes," Letty said bitterly, installing herself on one of the seats, "and yet she is nowhere in sight, is she?"

"I believe," said Miss Cosgrove, scooting next to Letty as Jacques climbed in and sat across from them, "that she stopped to talk to Mrs. Simmons for a moment as we were leaving."

Jacques left the the coach door open for Aunt Emily to enter whenever she arrived.

"Then three quarters of an hour was *not* an overestimation," said Letty with a great sigh. "Mrs. Simmons is the greatest chatterbox."

"Surely it will not be that long," Jacques said, "however long it may *feel* to you. I, for one, am grateful to be outside where the temperature is much more comfortable and the noise less oppressive."

Letty frowned. "*You* may prefer the sound of carriage wheels and yelling coachmen to musical instruments and people conversing, but *I* surely do not."

Jacques encountered Miss Cosgrove's smile, peeping at the corner of her lips. Letty had a point, after all.

"What is that noise?" Letty said, perking up and straining an ear. "It sounds ominous."

A distant, muffled din sounded. "It is only the traffic, Letty," said Jacques with an amused smile at her. "A valiant attempt at an excuse to return to the ballroom, but fruitless, I'm afraid."

Letty paid him no heed. "Do you hear it? It is getting louder."

Miss Cosgrove stilled, and Jacques watched her listen, with her eyes on the open door.

And Letty was right. Jacques could hear it—a cacophony of voices increasing in volume and, he could only guess, proximity.

The sound of glass breaking met his ears. He frowned and rose from his seat, hanging on the door frame to peer down the street. Torch-bearing men led the mob, bearing down the street determinedly. His eyes widened, and he stepped back into the coach.

"A riot," he said, shutting the door soundly. "We must hope they pass by and leave us in peace."

Letty's face went white. "Surely they wouldn't harm us?"

Jacques grimaced. He didn't wish to frighten her, but nor did he wish to mislead her. "I will do everything in my power to keep you both safe. But when hungry people combine in a mob, they become desperate and destructive. And the people are *very* hungry."

Shouting, stomping, and chanting drew nearer, and Jacques watched Miss Cosgrove look through the carriage window, taking a deep breath as if to still her nerves. He sincerely hoped that she would not succumb to fear—Letty would be looking to her and Jacques for direction and comfort, and if Letty saw Miss Cosgrove in terror, it would only add to her own.

Traffic had stopped in the street, and the sound of carriage doors shutting and horses pawing and neighing nervously could be heard through the coach windows.

Cecilia squinted as she continued looking through the window. "Good heavens," she said in alarm, "that boy could be killed if he remains there."

Lord Moulinet moved beside her to look through the window, and their shoulders rested against each other. Outside the carriage, a slender young page boy looked about in fear, as if searching for a place to hide. The doors to the Simmons' house were shut and the liveried servants who had stood by the doors nowhere to be seen, no doubt protecting the house from a possible invasion.

"You are right." Jacques moved to the coach door, opening it swiftly and calling to the page. "In here, young man!"

The page boy spun around and, seeing Jacques, rushed over to the door, hopping gracefully up the stairs and into the carriage as the sound of more breaking glass assailed their ears.

His breath came quickly as he sat down next to Jacques. "Thank you," he said, gasping. "You have saved my life."

A woman screamed in a nearby carriage, and Jacques looked through the window and swore softly. "They are lighting things aflame wherever they can."

The fear within the carriage was tangible, and Jacques's mind raced, trying to prepare in the event that their own coach was lit on fire. The page boy would hardly be an asset in such a situation—he was slender and almost delicate-looking.

Letty grabbed Miss Cosgrove's hand.

"Are we going to die?" Letty said tearfully.

Jacques grimaced and reached over to put his hand atop Miss Cosgrove's and Letty's hands, feeling his heart jump as he did so.

"Decidedly not." He smiled teasingly at Letty, hoping that it would act as a calming influence, showing Letty that he was in control of the situation—even if he wasn't. "If the mob requires a sacrifice from the four of us, I shall offer myself. This world cannot be allowed to go on without Miss Letitia Broussard. Or Miss Cecilia Cosgrove." He glanced at the boy next to him. "Or..." he raised his brows in a question.

The young man shifted in his seat. "Vaughan," he said, clearing his throat. "David Vaughan." His voice, like his figure, had a slightly feminine quality to it.

The sounds of the mob reached their peak, and Letty turned her face into Miss Cosgrove's shoulder, muttering something unintelligible.

A chaos of shouts—angry from the marching men, fearful from those confined to their carriages—continued for a full minute that seemed to stretch an hour. The three others all seemed frozen, barely breathing, while Jacques willed his breath to come evenly through his flared nostrils.

The mob passed by the coach without incident, and Miss Cosgrove let out a large breath of relief, pressing her eyelids shut as though she were praying.

Jacques watched her and grimaced his understanding. "We are safe," he said.

Letty's grasp on Miss Cosgrove's hand loosened. "I was sure we would all be killed."

"After I reassured you that I wouldn't allow such a thing?" said Jacques, feigning deep offense. "How very deflating is your opinion of me."

Letty laughed. "What could you possibly do to stop a mob of hundreds? Even with Mr. Vaughan's help?" She looked at Mr.

Vaughan, as if to see whether she had offended him. Letty's head tilted to the side, and her eyes narrowed.

She shot up suddenly in her seat, and her jaw hung agape.

Jacques looked to Miss Cosgrove, but she looked every bit as nonplussed as he felt.

"I know you," said Letty with bursting energy. "I had heard rumors, of course, but never did I think to see you for myself, much less to find myself sitting in the same carriage as you! How very famous!"

Mr. Vaughan's mouth twisted to the side to stop a smile.

"What ever are you talking about, Letty?" Miss Cosgrove asked.

Letty looked at Mr. Vaughan, who nodded, as if to grant permission.

"This," Letty said in a proud voice, "is not a page boy, but rather the glorious and brilliant Lady Caroline Lamb."

Jacques's jaw hung slack as he stared at the young person next to him, who was wearing an amused smile. She wagged her eyebrows at Miss Cosgrove.

"And very much indebted I am to all of you," she said, "for granting me sanctuary."

They were telling the truth, Letty and the young page—or Lady Caroline, rather. Jacques had seen Lady Caroline only once since his arrival in London, with her close-cropped hair, pleasing smile, and sprightly figure. Dressed as she was, though, it had been easy to miss the familiar features. Who would have assumed such a costume, after all?

The coach door opened, and Aunt Emily climbed in. "Praise be to heaven," she said. "I have been fretting this past fifteen minutes that you had all been injured by the mob, but on no account would the Simmons' servants allow the doors to be opened, so I was obliged"— she stopped upon seeing Lady Caroline and looked to Jacques for an explanation.

"Ah, yes," he said, glancing at Lady Caroline. "This young..." he trailed off, unsure how to continue. Did Lady Caroline wish to keep her identity a secret?

"Lady Caroline Lamb, madam," she said with a regal nod, "and very pleased to make your acquaintance."

Aunt Emily stilled in the act of depositing herself on the seat with Letty and Miss Cosgrove, staring.

"Lady Caroline," said Jacques with a twitch at the corner of his mouth, "this is my aunt, Mrs. Emily Broussard, her daughter, Miss Letitia Broussard, and Mrs. Broussard's niece, Miss Cecilia Cosgrove."

Aunt Emily's mouth hung agape for a moment as she nodded absently at the introduction. The look of confusion on her face was comical. She blinked a few times and closed her mouth.

"We are honored, my lady," she said, "and we would be more than happy to convey you to your lodgings?" She looked a question at Jacques. "My niece lives not far, in Belport Street, but it would be our pleasure to take you anywhere you wish first—"

"Belport Street?" said Lady Caroline in a curious voice. A mischievous smile appeared on her delicate lips. "That will do just fine, thank you. I shall not trouble you to convey me home—you have done more than enough to assist me this evening, after all—but Belport Street is very near my destination. In fact," she said, tilting her head to the side and putting a finger to her mouth, "if it won't be too great a trouble, Miss Cosgrove, might I step inside your home for a few minutes? I believe I am not expected at my rendezvous for another half hour or more."

Miss Cosgrove's brows went up, but she nodded quickly. "Of course, you are more than welcome."

Jacques suppressed a smile. What would the Cosgroves say to seeing her step inside with a page boy? The night could hardly have become stranger than it was.

The coach pulled forward, and Lady Caroline filled the unwieldy silence with questions for the Broussards and Jacques. She seemed very interested in their French heritage and Jacques's story of emigration. He gave the same answers he had always given—explaining how it came to be that he and his father had escaped to England with all of their belongings, when so many others had come with only the clothes on their backs.

He breathed a silent sigh of relief as the coach pulled in front of the Cosgroves' townhome. Would he ever get used to telling his fabricated story? It had enough truth in it, to be sure, but enough untruth to make him wriggle, even after twenty years.

He disliked watching Miss Cosgrove rise from her seat to leave. He had become uncomfortably conscious of how much he desired to prolong any time with her, and he found himself particularly reluctant to watch her go after the terrifying episode they had just experienced.

"I shall walk you both to the door," said Jacques, rising from his seat while feeling annoyed at his seeming inability to leave things well alone. "There is enough mischief afoot in town that great care should be taken."

"What a splendid idea," said Lady Caroline.

Miss Cosgrove bid her aunt and cousin farewell as Jacques opened the coach door and stepped down onto the flagstones below. He looked up and down the street for any sign of danger, but the only sound was of carriage wheels.

He handed down Lady Caroline, followed by Miss Cosgrove, whose slender, gloved hand seemed at home within his own.

The three of them walked abreast, with Jacques falling behind as they approached the door.

Lady Caroline looked at Jacques with the hint of a smile and then put a hand to the crimson livery she wore. She let out an exasperated sigh. "I think I have left the note I am delivering in the coach. Excuse me—I won't be but a moment." She nodded at them both and turned back to the coach.

Jacques's eyes narrowed. He was tolerably sure that Lady Caroline had never had a note in her possession. Had she seen through

Jacques so quickly that she was simply trying to provide time alone for him and Miss Cosgrove?

Miss Cosgrove fidgeted with the reticule in her hands, watching Lady Caroline. Jacques had the distinct impression that she was avoiding his eyes.

Was she embarrassed? He had wondered whether she had felt regret at the familiar conversation they had shared at dinner a few nights ago—at being found in tears. The last thing he wished was for her to put her mask back on.

She finally looked to him, the light of the sconces on the doorstep reflecting in her eyes. "An evening to remember, I think," he said.

She smiled responsively. "Yes, indeed." She glanced at the coach. "I think you have forever secured Lady Caroline's benevolence."

"Yes," he said, "if only I could achieve the same with you."

Her eyes shot to his, and she seemed to tense until meeting his teasing smile.

She relaxed and looked at him enigmatically. "Perhaps if you had rescued me, as you did her, from impending death?"

He chuckled, meeting her eyes. "A gross oversight on my part." Few things gave him as much pleasure as bantering with Miss Cosgrove.

Lady Caroline returned, slightly breathless, looking back and forth between the two of them with approval. She expressed her gratitude to Jacques a final time, and Miss Cosgrove bid him a smiling adieu.

He watched as they disappeared into the house, knowing he was walking a very precarious tightrope: the force of his growing attraction pulling him to one side, his desire to be true to his identity pulling him to the other side, and an abyss of potential ruin below.

9

When Cecilia and Lady Caroline entered the Cosgrove house, Cecilia felt almost lightheaded at the strange events of the night—at the knowledge that she was to entertain Lady Caroline Lamb herself for she didn't know how long.

The footman they met in the entry hall looked at them askance, particularly upon hearing Lady Caroline speak in a decidedly feminine voice.

She wanted nothing so much as some tea and cold meat and cheese —"For I missed dinner entirely this evening, you know."

Cecilia rang the bell, and within a matter of minutes, they were seated in the parlor together, Cecilia making and pouring the tea, while Lady Caroline talked between bites of food.

Cecilia had heard much about the lively woman in front of her— everyone had, of course. Between her marriage to William Lamb and the scandal with Lord Byron, she was one of the most gossiped about women in society. Contrary to Cecilia's expectations, too, she was very open about Lord Byron and their falling out. Cecilia found herself fascinated by Lady Caroline and the life she lived.

When an opportunity presented itself, Cecilia found the courage to ask, "But why dress up as a man? You are such a beautiful and accomplished woman that I find it incredible."

Lady Caroline smiled impishly amidst chewing and then swallowed a sip of tea. "It is diverting, of course," she said, "but also entirely liberating. As Lady Caroline, people expect something very particular when they see me. But as a man—even a page boy—I am allowed a great deal of license. I am entirely free to act as I please."

Cecilia's mouth broke into an understanding smile. "You manage to make it a very attractive prospect."

Lady Caroline shrugged. "If you harbor any doubts, the only solution is to try it yourself sometime."

Cecilia's heartbeat quickened at the thought. "But what if one is discovered?"

Lady Caroline lifted both hands with her palms up in a careless gesture. "I have given up fretting over the things that are said about me. I have found that, no matter what I do, I am condemned by some. So I may as well enjoy myself, don't you think?"

Cecilia's eyes widened slowly. She could hardly imagine such indifference to opinion—such freedom. Lady Caroline did what she pleased, without regard for who praised her for it or who criticized her for it.

Even now, as Cecilia watched her with awe, Lady Caroline sipped her tea unconcernedly, dressed as a page boy—as though there were nothing more natural in the world.

She was truly free.

Cecilia looked at the long-sleeved muslin Anaïs had set out for the day and thought of what the maid might say if she were asked to dress her mistress up as a page. Or did Lady Caroline dress herself for such ventures?

A smile played across Cecilia's lips as she imagined herself dressed in such clothing. Would she be recognized? She wished she had thought to ask Lady Caroline what other costumes she had donned—had she ever dressed as a gentleman?

Anaïs knocked and entered, holding a freshly laundered fichu and a letter. "For you, *mademoiselle.*"

Cecilia took the letter and glanced at the seal, which she had no difficulty recognizing as Lady Caroline's. She broke it open and read hungrily.

My Dear Miss Cosgrove,

Permit me to express to you my deep gratitude for your kindness toward me two nights since. You took me in—a stranger—and you fed me and entertained me with delightful conversation. I hope that you will allow me to call upon you tomorrow to convey my thanks in person.

Your affectionate friend,

Caro

Cecilia smiled as she folded the letter up. She couldn't pretend not to be flattered that Lady Caroline wished to continue their acquaintance. She liked the woman. Despite all the rumors of her obsession with Byron—her madness for him—she had achieved something Cecilia found herself coveting very much: indifference.

Cecilia was exhausted from months of seeking to satisfy the expectations of others. What she wouldn't give to be free of the burden of society's opinion! It seemed an impossible dream.

Cecilia paused at the doorway of the breakfast room, fortifying herself at the prospect of breakfasting with her parents.

Her father was already halfway through his plate of mutton, her mother pouring herself a cup of tea, and Tobias nowhere to be seen.

Naturally. Tobias had the freedom to go where he wanted, whenever he wanted, with no questions asked of him.

She sighed and took her seat at the table, causing her father to look up.

"Ah, my little Cecy," he said affectionately.

She smiled back at him, placing a napkin on her lap. She liked when he called her by her nickname.

He raised his brows at her enigmatically. "You have been quite busy, haven't you? Wooing marquesses and vicomtes and heaven knows who else!"

Cecilia's cheeks burned. "You're mistaken, Papa. I haven't woo'd"— she said the word with a touch of revulsion —"Lord Moulinet. Or anyone, for that matter."

"Indeed," said his wife, "Cecilia has assured me that she is quite set on having the marquess."

Cecilia's brows snapped together. Her mother must have imagined Cecilia's side of the conversation. She felt her anger rising while her hands began to shake slightly with nerves.

"Perhaps you are misremembering, Mama. And who knows? Lord Retsford's affections might transfer without warning. It would be entirely consistent with his reputation, which I admit gives me pause. He is quite old, too." Seeing her parents' displeased expressions, she felt the need to provide justification for her feelings.

"Just the other day, Letty and I came upon him in the park, and he seemed to take no small interest in her." She felt her nerves compelling her to keep speaking, as if it might delay the reactions she feared.

Her father set his wrists down on the table edge, a fork in one hand and a knife in the other, with an expression of alarm. "Letitia Broussard?" He scoffed. "The marquess isn't fool enough to trade you for *her*."

"She is very agreeable, Papa, and—"

"And as for his being old," her father continued, seemingly oblivious to her speaking, "why should that concern you? It only means you will outlive him to enjoy the benefits of the marquessate without the *duties* of a wife."

Cecilia's cheeks flamed red.

"Or perhaps," she said, unable to contain herself, "I wish to marry someone whose wife I *enjoy* being, rather than someone whose death I look forward to with impatience."

Both her mother and father looked at her with bemused expressions, but her father's jaw set, and the vein in his forehead protruded. "Or perhaps," he said in a biting tone, "you would do well to remember that you are still reliant on *me* for a dowry."

Cecilia's nostrils flared. "You would refuse me my portion if I marry anyone of less rank than a marquess?" She blew air through her nose as she stood, walking to the breakfast room door, where she turned her head to say, "Surely you are capable of coming up with another way to force your will upon others, Papa. The tactic is hardly original."

She closed the door behind her, chest heaving and eyes squeezed shut. It had been quite some time since she had been angry enough to throw one of the fits her family knew her for.

She had known just how to obtain what she wanted since she had been a little girl. If she was ever told no, if her will was ever crossed, she had but to fly into a rage for her father to capitulate.

But the anger coursing through her was different today. It was an anger bred of exhaustion, helplessness, and discontent. It was anger directed at herself as much as at her parents, for she knew that she had played no small part in the expectations which had grown up like weeds around her. She had watered those weeds, encouraging her parents to expect a brilliant match for her, ensuring that the possibilities afforded by her allure and beauty never left the forefront of their thoughts.

And now she was reaping the rewards of her own vanity.

She stalked down the corridor, clenching and unclenching her fists, suppressing a desire to scream.

The bell of the front door rang, and she stopped, listening.

Lady Caroline's now-familiar voice met her ears, muffled though it was.

Cecilia had not expected her so early in the day. But Lady Caroline was flighty and eccentric enough that it hardly surprised her.

Cecilia's eyes lit up with energy, her fingers still shaking with suppressed frustration. Who would better understand her predicament than Lady Caroline?

By the time the footman closed the door to the morning room behind him, leaving Cecilia and Lady Caroline to themselves, Cecilia was nearly in control of her emotions. Or so she thought.

"My oh my," said Lady Caroline, her head moving from side to side as she looked at Cecilia, "you are even *more* beautiful in a rage. What has happened to make your eyes so bright, and your cheeks that particular shade of pink?"

Cecilia let out a large breath and shut her eyes. "Only that I am so tired. So very tired"— she punctuated each word with a pause —"of being what everyone wants me to be." She looked at Lady Caroline and smiled wryly. "I have found myself daydreaming of page boys and livery more than once since the other night." She laughed softly. "Words I never thought I would say."

Lady Caroline tilted her head to the side and tossed her shoulders up. "And what is keeping you from doing it?"

Cecilia frowned and then gave a light shrug. "Fear, I suppose."

Lady Caroline made a dismissive hand gesture. "That is no reason at all!" She paused and a hint of a smile tugged at the corner of her mouth. "What if we did it together?"

Cecilia's brows shot up. "And where would we go?"

The mischievous smile grew. "Where have you always wished to go but never dared as a woman?"

Cecilia let out a puff of air. She had never considered it because there had been no utility in doing so. But surely the options were not as limitless as Lady Caroline implied. "As a page boy?"

Lady Caroline frowned a moment. "We need not dress as page boys. I chose that costume for a very particular reason." She suppressed a smile at whatever memory her words had triggered. "We can be gentlemen if you wish."

Cecilia's pulse quickened. Gentlemen? Her skin tingled.

It wouldn't be difficult to obtain some of Tobias's clothes. Surely they wouldn't be the snug fit they were on *him*, but...

"A prize fight," Cecilia said suddenly. "I wish to see a prize fight."

Lady Caroline looked at her with approbation. "Then a prize fight we shall see." She stood and began pacing, her fingers softly rubbing her dainty lips. "I will discover where the next one is taking place, and we shall go." She turned to Cecilia. "It will be quite an adventure, I think."

Cecilia swallowed, but she couldn't stifle a smile.

Freedom.

She would experience one night of freedom.

10

The open landau rumbled down Oxford Street, and Jacques had to raise his voice to be heard by Letty and Miss Cosgrove, who both held a number of bandboxes in their laps.

"Have you any other commissions to fulfill?" he said, his ears ringing from the hustle and bustle of town traffic.

Letty had begged him to accompany them on their shopping expedition. She needn't have begged, though.

Jacques was painfully aware of his own eagerness for any excuse to spend time in Miss Cosgrove's company.

She was still an enigma to him, sometimes open and charmingly unaffected, at other times disappointingly similar to any other young woman whose company he might have passed time in.

"I, for one," said Miss Cosgrove, fanning herself lightly, "could use some kind of refreshment."

"Capital idea," said Jacques. He frowned. "Though I confess I have no knowledge of where we might go for such a thing."

Miss Cosgrove tilted her head as she looked at him and smiled. "Have you never had an ice from Gunter's, then?"

Jacques shook his head.

"Oh," Letty chimed in with excitement, "nor have I, but I have heard it is excessively fashionable—and truly delicious. Let us go there, if you please!" She clasped her hands in front of her chest and looked to Jacques with large, pleading eyes.

Jacques chuckled. Whoever Letty married, he would need to immune himself to such soulful appeals unless he wished to find himself under the girl's thumb his entire life. "I wouldn't dare refuse you."

He looked a question at Miss Cosgrove who said, "Berkeley Square, then," and Jacques called out to the coachman.

"Now comes the difficult part," said Miss Cosgrove with a glint of teasing in her eye. "Deciding upon a flavor."

As she detailed the different options available to them, Jacques leaned in across the seats of the landau to hear her better, smiling as he watched her describing the merits of the *glace de crême aux fromages* against those of the orange flower flavor.

When the landau stopped in Berkeley Square, Jacques hopped down, looking at the glinting windows of Gunter's where confectionery jars of every color sat beckoning to passing shoppers. Not even a minute had passed before a waiter rushed over to the carriage, asking how he could serve them.

As the ladies sat in the carriage enjoying their refreshment, Jacques stood against the wrought-iron railing surrounding the square, spooning the fast-melting ice cream into his mouth contentedly. A young boy and his mother walked by, the boy staring wide-eyed at the parmesan-flavored ice and informing his mother that he wanted just such a treat.

Jacques smiled indulgently at the child. If the seven-year-old Jacques, running errand after errand for Monsieur le Comte in the tense streets of Montreuil could see himself now, he would never have believed his eyes.

The life he and his father had created in England was easy and serene, nothing like the one they had left in France more than twenty years ago, nothing like the first moments in Dover where the specter of death had been their welcome. One of the first things Jacques had done on English soil had been to help his father dig a grave by moonlight in the nearest churchyard. The memory still chilled him, bringing the hairs on the back of his neck to a stand.

A raised voice sounded across the street, and Jacques pushed himself off the railing to see where it was coming from. A pleading voice in heavily-accented English responded, and Miss Cosgrove shifted in her seat, eyeing the source of the fray with distaste and unease.

Jacques walked around the landau to see what the cause of the disturbance was.

A woman, dressed in a drab brown dress with dirt clinging to the fraying threads at the hem, was surrounded by three children, begging passers-by for two pence. The smartly-dressed waiter from Gunter's pointed vigorously down the street, raising his voice to demand the family's departure.

"Whatever were they thinking, coming here of all places?" Miss Cosgrove said, watching them warily from the corner of her eye.

"I don't know, but perhaps we should leave?" Letty said.

It was strange indeed to see *émigrés* in this part of town.

Jacques's jaw clenched as he regarded one of the young children the woman had in tow. He couldn't have been more than six years old, and his blackened clothing and skin left no room for doubt that he was employed as a chimney sweep. Had Jacques's circumstances been different, he might have looked very much the same as the sooty boy.

He felt a weight drop into the pit of his stomach as a drip of cheese-flavored ice ran down his hand. He was no better than that family; his origins were the same. And yet he stood, lighthearted, eating an ice that likely cost as much as the family's wages for the week.

The young boy licked his lips with awed eyes as he watched another waiter carry two goblets of ice to the carriage in front of the landau Jacques stood next to. The occupants were speaking in low voices as they watched the spectacle before them.

Jacques frowned. He couldn't stand idly by, pretending to belong with the high-born people who surrounded him, looking down upon the young family of *émigrés*. *They* were his countrymen, his real equals; not the whispering, censuring *beau-monde* he feigned to belong to—the ones who viewed the family's mere presence as a direct threat to the comfortable existence they felt entitled to.

He glanced at Miss Cosgrove, with her fear and aversion; and Letty with her wary vigilance.

Taking in a large breath, he handed his ice to Letty and, asking her to hold it, stepped across the street.

"I will send for the constable immediately if you refuse to leave, ma'am," the waiter said.

The woman responded in French, clearly not comprehending the man's words or the danger she stood in. The last thing the poor family needed was an encounter with a constable.

"Excuse me," Jacques said to the waiter.

Upon seeing who had interrupted him, the waiter's expression morphed from one of black-browed threat to one of polite questioning. He bowed to Jacques. "How may I serve you, sir?"

Jacques looked at the waiter for a moment and then crouched down in front of the children, who were regarding him with uncertainty and fear.

"What flavor of ice would you like?" Jacques asked them in French.

Their eyes widened in concert, and they looked up at their mother with unsure but hopeful eyes, as if it might be a trick.

She looked to Jacques, the same mistrust reflected in her own gaze.

"I, too, am an *émigré*," he said, wishing he could say more.

She kept her gaze on him, evaluating whether he posed a threat. He smiled sadly and then nodded at her children to tell him what they desired.

"Une glace aux amandes!" said the soot-covered young boy who had reminded Jacques of himself. The boy glanced at his mother and added in a subdued tone, *"S'il vous plaît, Monsieur."*

The other two children chimed in with a wish for elderberry and lavender, and Jacques smiled, watching their eyes light up with anticipation. Had they ever had such a treat?

Surely the ice would be a welcome change from the plain, boiled potatoes they likely ate every day.

The waiter cleared his throat. "Sir," he said in English, "I can send someone for the constable if they are troubling you."

Jacques looked at the man, whose light sneer intensified as he sent a sidelong glance at the family. He shook his head. "I would like to order four more ices."

One of the waiter's brows went up. "For them, sir?" He indicated the family with his head.

"Yes, of course," Jacques replied. "One *glace aux amandes*, one lavender, one elderberry..."

Jacques looked to the mother, who was smiling sadly at her delighted children.

He was aware of the many eyes upon them, of the raised brows and jaws agape in the carriages lined up along the street. With a hint of consternation, Jacques noted Lord Retsford and Miss Fletcher, the former stepping down from a curricle behind the landau, his eyes on Jacques.

"And for you, madame?" Jacques said in French again, pulling his eyes back to the *émigrés*.

Her brows went up as she met his eyes, and he nodded to reassure her. "Please allow me to offer this small gesture to a fellow countrywoman."

She shot an uneasy glance at the waiter and said, speaking to Jacques, "Another lavender, then, if you please." She hazarded a grateful smile at him.

Jacques relayed the message to the waiter, who nodded tightly, saying, "Very good, sir," before walking into Gunter's.

Jacques led the family across the street toward the landau, hoping to provide less opportunity for the gawking and gaping that was occurring. He felt surprisingly collected, despite the probable foolishness of what he was doing.

He looked up as he approached the landau and saw Miss Cosgrove looking down at him and the *émigrés* with distaste. He frowned and suppressed a sigh. She wouldn't understand what he was doing.

"I think you will be more comfortable here," he said to the children, ignoring the disapproval he was courting, as the three came to stand awkwardly in front of the railing. If their coarse clothing and dirty skin hadn't immediately betrayed how little they belonged, their wide-eyed stares and ever-shifting feet would have.

"Jacques," Letty whispered in an urgent voice.

He sighed, excused himself to the family, and walked over to his cousin.

"What are you doing?" she said.

He shrugged, feeling annoyed that he was expected to account for his behavior to his young cousin. "I am helping some people who stand in need."

"With ice?" Letty said doubtfully.

"Why not? They will likely appreciate it much more than any of us do."

"Perhaps," said Miss Cosgrove, sending a false smile to the people staring at them and speaking through lightly clenched teeth, "but we are attracting a good deal of attention, and I cannot think it seemly to be fraternizing with complete strangers—and *émigrés*, no less."

Jacques's jaw shifted, and his muscles tensed. "Then it cannot be seemly for you to be seen with me, can it? I, too, am an *émigré*."

Miss Cosgrove frowned. "Yes, but that is different."

He raised his brows. Little did she realize how wrong her words were. He stared at her for a moment. "Have I endangered your safety? Or is it your reputation you fear for?" He couldn't keep the bite from his voice.

She blinked rapidly, her eyes downcast as her cheeks turned red.

Feeling a sting of guilt, Jacques explained, "They are poor; they are not beasts."

"I have never spoken to an *émigré*," said Letty, eyeing them with a spark of interest. She pursed her lips and then stood, putting a hand out to Jacques for assistance down from the landau.

He shuffled over quickly and took her hand in his.

Letty walked over to the family, addressing them in her indifferent French with a kind smile. Shy at first, the children responded to her with short, monosyllabic answers.

Jacques's mouth turned up in a half-smile. It warmed his heart to see Letty stepping into unknown territory, heedless of the scandalized eyes which watched her.

Miss Cosgrove cleared her throat, and Jacques looked up. Her hand was extended toward him, like Letty's had been, waiting for him to assist her down the steps.

His heart jumped to his throat as he handed her down from the landau.

She nodded her thanks to him and strode over to the mother, asking her name and inquiring in pretty French whether she was enjoying the ice. The mother responded with bulging eyes and short, jerky nods—she could hardly have looked more surprised if she had been approached by the Prince Regent himself.

Jacques walked over, feeling strangely light and happy. Miss Cosgrove was stooped down in front of the youngest child, a little girl of no more than three, asking her name.

"Maurine Géroux," the young girl replied, wiping her dirt-streaked cheek with the back of the fist which clutched her spoon tightly. With her other hand, she extended the goblet of ice toward Miss Cosgrove. "Would you like some, miss? It is delicious."

Miss Cosgrove glanced at Jacques with her suppressed smile and a touched expression. Their eyes met in mutual amusement, and Jacques felt a quiver of joy at the shared moment.

Turning back to the young Maurine, she said, "That is very kind of you, indeed, but I think that *you* should have the pleasure of eating every last bite."

Jacques smiled as Maurine beamed and spooned a heaping serving of the ice into her mouth.

"What interesting company you keep, Miss Cosgrove." The interjecting voice held a touch of derision.

Jacques stood and turned, coming face to face with Lord Retsford, whose eyes raked over the *émigré* family and then landed on Jacques. "Pray introduce me to your cousin who"— he scanned Jacques's clothing from his top hat down to his boots —"is from the country, I take it."

One of Jacques's eyebrows went up.

Miss Cosgrove came up next to him, saying, "Lord Retsford, this is le Vicomte de Moulinet, a cousin to *my* cousins, the Broussards. Lord Moulinet, this is the Marquess of Retsford."

The marquess inclined his head ever-so-slightly as Jacques bowed.

"You have a familiar air about you, Moulinet," said the marquess. "Have we perhaps met before?"

"I think not, my lord," said Jacques. "Unless you spend any time in Devon? I do not often come to town."

"Ah yes," Lord Retsford said with an amused half-smile, his eyes moving again to Jacques's clothing. "That much is apparent." He looked at the French family, who had all finished their goblets of ice and were standing awkwardly behind Jacques, Letty, and Miss Cosgrove. "At least you seem to have found your fellows here in town."

Jacques felt his blood pulsing in his veins. Why the man had taken him in such obvious dislike, he didn't know. That it had something to do with Miss Cosgrove, he was fairly certain; the marquess seemed territorial. "I have found," Jacques said with false amiability, "that, here in town, rank is a poor indicator of how agreeable I will find someone's company."

He tipped his hat at the marquess and, with a civil smile, walked back to the French family, giving a handful of coins to the mother and wishing her a good day, while ignoring the blood pounding in his ears.

"Good heavens," said Miss Cosgrove when Jacques came to stand next to her and Letty. "How did you wrong Lord Retsford that he should behave toward you in such a manner?"

"I imagine," Jacques said with a shrug, "that it doesn't please him to see you in my company."

"Well of all the things," said Miss Cosgrove, incensed. "And him escorting Miss Fletcher here alone!" She scoffed.

Was she jealous? Or merely upset at the double standard?

He assisted both the ladies into the landau, seating himself across from them and signaling the driver to return them to the Broussard residence.

"Thank you—both of you," he said, "for your kindness to that family."

"Little Maurine was a darling," Miss Cosgrove said with a laugh. "I should never have guessed I would enjoy talking to such people, but they were very gracious and amiable." She glanced at Jacques, who was watching her through slightly narrowed eyes, and smiled widely. "And it *was* somewhat invigorating to flout the opinions of all those watching."

Jacques chuckled weakly. "You will have made a new fashion. No doubt on your next visit to Gunter's, you will see poor men lined up to receive ice from the ladies and gentlemen in their carriages."

He was glad that Miss Cosgrove had condescended to speak with the Géroux family. He would have been disappointed if she had maintained the distancing attitude she had first assumed. But something was shifting inside of her. He could sense it. She wasn't the same person he had met at the ball on his first evening in town.

But to Miss Cosgrove, talking to such people was simple benevolence and charity—a brief step down from her proper place.

For Jacques, it was an acknowledgment of his origins, of where he belonged. Nothing separated him from looking or acting like the

Géroux family except happenstance and luck. He had done nothing to deserve what he now had.

He was torn between two worlds—and he would never be comfortable in either. He had lived too long as nobility to view a return to the life and misery of a poor man with anything but great misgiving—even dread; but he was an impostor in the world in which he now lived, never certain how much people valued *him* or simply the title they assumed he possessed.

He wasn't sure how to continue with the duplicity.

❧ 11 ❧

I t hadn't taken Cecilia longer than two minutes to look at her brother's clothing, lying before her on the bed, and realize that she would need assistance to put it on. Her hair, too, would need arranging, or else it would give her away. Thus it was that she had been forced to take Anaïs into her confidence.

But the maid, so far from being scandalized, had looked overjoyed to be involved in such a hazardous and scandalous undertaking.

Cecilia's heart fluttered at the thought of what she was about to do. It was pure folly. And yet terribly invigorating.

The pantaloons she wore clung strangely to her legs, making her feel naked and exposed while also giving a sense of support and sturdiness she was unused to. The arms of her brother's coat were meant for much broader shoulders and thicker arms—seeing it on Cecilia, no one would assume that the coat was actually made by Stultz and fit Tobias like a glove. But it would do well enough for the night.

Cecilia's golden hair was all pinned atop her head—Anaïs had done a decent job of making it look even instead of lumpy. But they had agreed that it would be better to keep Tobias's top hat on.

Cecilia had no idea what to expect from a prize fight. Lady Caroline had simply instructed her to await word—and that word had come in the morning as Cecilia sat taking breakfast in her bed.

But the note, instructing Cecilia to be dressed and ready by two, was followed only an hour after by another note, informing her that the fight was delayed.

Disappointed but slightly relieved, Cecilia had been deciding whether to request her mother's chaperonage to a party when yet another note had arrived, requesting that Cecilia listen for Lady Caroline's carriage at eleven that evening.

"Voilà," said Anaïs, putting the finishing touches on the cravat. She handed Tobias's top hat to Cecilia, who put it gently on her head and turned to look at her reflection in the mirror.

She pulled her lips between her teeth to suppress a smile at the sight. Her complexion was free of any trace of makeup, save the burnt cork Anaïs had insisted upon using to darken and thicken Cecilia's brows. They looked unnaturally dark, but Anaïs assured her that the darkening was very necessary if she wished to go unrecognized.

Cecilia heard the faint sound of carriage wheels, and her heart skipped. Her father was at Brooks's and her mother had already retired for the evening. But Cecilia was nervous enough that she took the back staircase all the same.

She tilted her hat and bowed her head as she made her way down the stairs, hoping that, if any servants saw her, they would assume her to be Tobias.

She had no desire for her adventure to end before it ever began.

A stony-faced postilion opened the door of the chaise, and Cecilia climbed inside swiftly, anxious for the safety and anonymity of the closed carriage.

Lady Caroline clapped her hands upon seeing Cecilia. "Magnificent! What an adventure we shall have." Unlike Cecilia, Lady Caroline's clothing fit her tall, thin figure snugly.

"You look like a tulip of the *ton,*" Cecilia said with some envy. "I look like a country bumpkin wearing his older brother's clothing."

Lady Caroline's musical laugh sounded. "I have found it convenient to have a man's coat made to my measurements, though I have only used it on one other occasion." She smiled impishly. "In any case, the fight tonight will be well-attended, I think, so we must channel our very best acting skill if we are to avoid being found out. I have more experience than you in this, so if you find yourself in a pinch, allow me to do the talking."

Cecilia swallowed and nodded nervously.

"What name am I to give?" she asked.

Lady Caroline cocked an eyebrow. "Whatever name you fancy, of course. Tonight is about forgetting everything in your life that weighs you down or frustrates you. Tonight, you are free." She punctuated the last words with a pause, grinning widely.

Cecilia laughed shakily and pursed her smiling lips in thought. "George Goodwin," she said decidedly, and Lady Caroline nodded her acceptance of the name.

"And I," Lady Caroline said, "shall be Theophilus Faulkner."

Cecilia suppressed a laugh and then nodded formally, touching her hat softly and saying, "Pleased to make your acquaintance, Mr. Faulkner."

If it hadn't been for the constant stream of conversation Lady Caroline engaged her in, Cecilia thought she might have been sick by the time they arrived at the Harford, where the fight was set to take place. Her heart was beating double its regular speed and her hands were clammy. The only positive to the strong bout of nerves attacking her was that the sweat on her forehead seemed to keep her hat on more securely.

The low rumbling of conversation met their ears as the chaise came to a halt. Cecilia peeked through the chaise window and took in a steadying breath. Hordes of men—of both gentle and lower birth—surrounded a wooden platform on the wide green, lit with torches on all sides.

"Why is the fight taking place at night?" she said, still peering through the window. "Do they not normally occur in daylight?"

"Well, yes, normally they do. And it *was* planned for this afternoon near Hampstead, but apparently the magistrate received word. Fortunately, I was able to discover the new time and location." She held Cecilia's eyes, her hazel eyes alight with anticipation. "Are you ready?"

Cecilia nodded.

Lady Caroline's excitement was contagious, and Cecilia felt her skin prickling with the expectation of an entirely novel experience as they stepped down onto the dirt road where the line of equipages sat. They walked toward the growing mass of people surrounding the platform, and it wasn't long before the platform had disappeared from Cecilia's view, crowded out by the heads and hats before her.

"You see Hurst?" Lady Caroline said. "He is the smaller one—just a young farmer from a little south of here, as I understand it. But he is the favorite."

"I can't see a thing," Cecilia said with a laugh, standing on her tiptoes. "You forget how tall you are."

Lady Caroline looked down at her and pursed her lips. "We must find a closer view."

They pushed their way through the crowd of sweating bodies, eliciting some frustrated exclamations, which made Cecilia light-headed with nerves. But, without fail, upon seeing who had jostled them, the men went silent. Most of them looked like villagers and were perhaps reluctant to take issue with Theophilus Faulkner and George Goodwin, gentlemen. Cecilia tried to adopt her most masculine expression.

There were a number of faces Cecilia recognized, though, and while one part of her wished to avoid them at all costs, the reckless part of her was tempted to test the limits of her disguise.

She felt her whole body buzz with excitement. She could only imagine the scene she would be causing if she had been there in her regular attire.

But she had no chaperone, no rules to follow, and nothing to draw undue attention to her. Tonight, there was no delicate dress to be minded as they traipsed through the crowd, and instead of the thin slippers that offered little protection from anyone accidentally treading on her feet, Tobias's boots were sturdy—if somewhat large. She felt giddy with excitement and freedom.

Lady Caroline managed to find them a place just a few rows from the platform. The conversation around them buzzed with predictions and observations about the two fighters, standing on the raised wooden planks. Men held tankards of spirits which filled the air with a bitter scent, sometimes overcome by the pungent smell of sweating bodies. It was simultaneously disgusting and exhilarating.

The sound of men talking reached a pitch when it was apparent the fight was about to begin.

Boyle was introduced to a host of cheers, followed by Hurst, for whom the cheers were almost deafening. Cecilia couldn't see how such a small figure could possibly compete against the bulky and towering Boyle. Surely it was impossible. And yet the crowd had made clear its prediction and preference.

The fight began, and silence reigned, only the shuffling of the fighters' feet and their uneven breathing filling the air. The atmosphere was electric.

Boyle seemed at first to be gaining the advantage, as several of his blows met their target. But as time passed, Boyle began to tire, where Hurst shifted his weight from one foot to the other in an energetic dance that thrilled the crowds.

Cecilia thought she had never felt so alive. She yelled with the men around her whenever Hurst seemed to be struggling, and she shouted with each blow he struck at Boyle. It was a feeling she could only describe as invincibility.

More than half an hour had passed when Hurst managed to strike an unanticipated blow straight to Boyle's jaw, sending the man down to the planks below. The crowd chanted, counting each second as Boyle struggled to raise himself from the platform.

Cheers erupted as the final second passed, and Hurst raised his sinewy arms in the air, victorious, as Cecilia and Lady Caroline embraced and cheered.

The tight spaces between them and the men surrounding them loosened slightly, as men at the outskirts began to disperse.

Cecilia looked around at the widely grinning faces which met her everywhere. Not far off, a small circle had formed around two men.

"They want more fighting," Lady Caroline said, tracking the line of Cecilia's gaze.

Cecilia continued scanning the crowd, still amazed that she was present for such an event.

Her breath hitched.

Lord Retsford stood a dozen feet away, in conversation with another gentleman.

"What is it?" Lady Caroline asked.

Cecilia let out a breath and held up her chin with a satisfied smile. "Nothing," she said. For once, she could be in the company of the marquess without having to worry about interacting with him.

Lady Caroline narrowed her eyes at Lord Retsford. "He is a determined suitor, isn't he?"

Cecilia nodded, but a smile quirked on her lips. "Not tonight."

"True." Lady Caroline smiled mischievously. "I have never liked the man."

"Nor I," Cecilia said. "I have half a mind to walk up to him and tell him what I really think of him."

"Well, I think you *should*," said Lady Caroline.

Cecilia let out a jeering laugh. "And what? Present my opinion with the compliments of George Goodwin, esquire?"

Lady Caroline shrugged and held Cecilia's gaze with a teasing challenge in her own. "Why ever not? Remember, tonight you are free."

Cecilia shivered at the thought, the exhilaration of the night pushing her to do what she would never otherwise entertain as an idea. She shut her eyes, imagining her hat flying off of her head, betraying her.

"No," she said, shaking her head rapidly. "I cannot."

Lady Caroline shrugged. "As you please. But I think we shall pass by him simply because we can."

Cecilia nodded, and Lady Caroline tucked her arm in Cecilia's, only to draw it away immediately and laugh at herself. "*That* is not something which lends to our credibility as gentlemen."

Cecilia laughed responsively, her eyes flitting to Lord Retsford, and they began walking toward him. He was frowning and speaking with clenched teeth to the man next to him.

Cecilia's stomach fluttered, and her skin tingled as they came abreast of him. Lady Caroline shifted their trajectory slightly so that she jostled the marquess as she passed by him, not even turning to offer an apology. She suppressed a smile and wagged an eyebrow at Cecilia.

Suddenly, Lady Caroline was shoved into Cecilia, sending them both scrambling to keep their footing, jostling others in the crowd around them.

Wide-eyed and with uneven breath, Cecilia turned to assess what had happened, putting a hand to stabilize her hat.

Lord Retsford stood, facing them with a sneer.

She felt herself freeze, her head light and dizzy. A number of people nearby stood watching.

Lord Retsford touched his hat with a slight nod in a mocking gesture. "Perhaps that will teach you to pay closer attention to your surroundings."

Lady Caroline nodded with a false smile. "Perhaps some surroundings don't merit our attention."

His nostrils flared.

A voice called out, "Fight him!"

And another, "Yes, teach the gawky man some manners!"

Cecilia swallowed, her mind feeling hazy. This couldn't be real. It had to be a dream.

"I think so," said Lord Retsford, taking off his hat and coat, which his friend assisted him with and then held in his hands.

Cecilia looked to Lady Caroline, who was finally demonstrating some of the fear that gripped Cecilia, with her wide-eyed, wary expression. If she fought, she would be beaten down within minutes. Or less.

Cecilia imagined conveying Lady Caroline home by herself, bloody and bruised; unconscious, even.

"I apologize, my lord," said Lady Caroline with a bow. "It will not happen again."

Lord Retsford smiled and shook his head, unbuttoning his shirt and tugging at his cravat to loosen it. "Too late, I am afraid. Are you a coward as well as an oaf?"

He wished to taunt her to anger, of course; he had no idea that he was challenging a woman—Lady Caroline Lamb, no less. But if she revealed her identity to quell the demand for a fight, their reputations would be ruined.

Cecilia felt nausea wash over her. Why had she agreed to come? The freedom she had felt earlier had evaporated.

She turned her head away as Lord Retsford pulled off his shirt and assumed a fighting stance, motioning for Lady Caroline to approach.

There was a growing crowd surrounding them—at least two dozen people, jeering; hungrily awaiting their entertainment.

A man broke through the ranks, striding up to Lord Retsford and punching him in the stomach. The marquess doubled over, gripping an arm to the point of contact.

Cecilia's eyes bulged as the man stepped back and said, "Bullying young men you're certain you can beat, Lord Retsford?"

Cecilia froze. It was Lord Moulinet.

She felt simultaneous terror and relief. What was he doing? And why? Had he recognized them?

Lord Retsford uncurled from his tucked position, staring at the vicomte. "I will more than gladly trade him for you, Moulinet."

Lord Moulinet bowed and began removing his hat, coat, and cravat, handing them to two men at the edge of the circle. He undid the buttons at his throat, and his shirt hung open. Cecilia blinked and averted her gaze. This was no time to be noticing the strength of the vicomte's chest. This was an unmitigated disaster.

"Come," Lady Caroline hissed, grabbing Cecilia's hand and pulling her from the center of the open circle to join the surrounding crowd.

Cecilia blinked rapidly and stepped back with her friend. The sound of the men in the crowd hurriedly placing their bets hummed in her ears.

Lord Moulinet faced Lord Retsford, both men with their leathery arms up, their hands balled into fists. They looked to be fairly evenly-matched, though Lord Retsford's height gave him a small advantage. His disdain for the vicomte, too, might prove a determining factor in the match.

Cecilia swallowed and squeezed her eyes shut. There was none of the exhilaration she had felt watching Hurst and Boyle—not when someone she knew was in the ring.

The first punches were thrown, but both men ducked and dodged them. Lord Retsford quickly attacked again, this time meeting his target with an uppercut to Lord Moulinet's jaw, who reeled and grabbed for the injury.

He quickly shook himself, though, and strode back over, sending a fist into Lord Retsford's stomach and then one to his cheek.

Cecilia felt sick with apprehension as she watched, fighting against a constant desire to hide her face in her hands as drops of blood went flying through the air. But she had to watch. She couldn't tear her eyes away.

The fighting continued, and Cecilia longed for it to end. Lord Retsford landed a throw in Lord Moulinet's stomach and sneered as he watched him heave. In his delight, he was unready for the crushing blow which Lord Moulinet sent flying into the marquess's other cheek.

Lord Retsford dropped to the ground, limp, and the crowd cheered.

Lord Moulinet stood back, watching the marquess, but twenty

seconds passed with no sign of movement. The crowd chanted the counting down of seconds, reaching thirty and breaking into applause and shouts of approbation, just as the marquess began to stir, pushing himself up. His brow was creased, his eyes blinking, and his head wobbling.

Lord Moulinet put out a hand to the marquess, but Lord Retsford looked at it and spat.

Lord Moulinet's hand lingered in the air for a moment, but the marquess showed no signs of noticing. "Have it your way," said the vicomte.

He walked over to the two men holding his clothing, taking his belongings and striding back through the circle toward Cecilia and Lady Caroline. His nose and lip were bleeding, and one of his eyes puffy and red.

Cecilia held her breath as he approached, but his eyes never landed on her or Lady Caroline.

"Come with me," he said sharply as he passed.

Cecilia looked to Lady Caroline, who nodded and turned to follow the vicomte.

They walked quickly, trying to keep pace with Lord Moulinet. Cecilia closed her eyes tightly for a moment, ashamed and half-hoping that the vicomte had not recognized them, that he was simply intent on instructing two naïve fellows on what they had done wrong.

They approached the long line of carriages and—finally—the vicomte turned around. He set down his belongings, his chest still bare, red from the blows it had sustained. The puffy pink and purple around his eye enhanced its piercing green color.

Cecilia averted her gaze, filling with guilt at the sight of his features marred with blood and bruising.

"I trust," he said, picking up his shirt and pulling it over his head, "that you have both had your fill of adventure for the night?"

Cecilia swallowed painfully, blinking as she felt her eyes sting, but she was saved the necessity of response by the approach of two gentlemen. "Shall we go, Moulinet?"

The vicomte's eyes rested on Cecilia and Lady Caroline for a moment. "You go on," he said. "I will accompany my new friends."

The gentlemen shrugged and moved on.

"Where is your carriage?" the vicomte said, buttoning up his shirt.

"Just down the line there," said Lady Caroline in a deeper tone than her usual voice, pointing to their chaise.

Cecilia exhaled, glad that Lady Caroline had spared her from having to respond. She didn't think she could manage pretending to be George Goodwin when she was feeling so much emotion. She knew how much Lord Moulinet hated affectation.

"Spare me the play acting, if you please, Lady Caroline," he said, shrugging on his coat and placing his hat atop his sweaty, brown locks. "Let us be on our way."

❧ 12 ❧

Jacques took deep strides toward the chaise Lady Caroline had indicated. He felt the vein in his neck pulsing with anger, but it was drowned out by the stinging and throbbing in his head and body.

Years of practice controlling his emotions were proving vital to keeping the frustration in check.

The folly of the two women walking behind him—attired in pantaloons, boots, and coats, of which some obviously belonged to Miss Cosgrove's brother—was incomprehensible to him.

He nodded to the postilion standing next to the chaise, and the man rushed to open the door.

Jacques smiled humorlessly at Lady Caroline and Cecilia, tilting his head. "I would give you a hand to assist you in, but I am afraid it would likely ruin the effect you are trying to achieve." He inclined his head to indicate their attire.

Miss Cosgrove swallowed visibly and avoided his gaze as she stepped into the carriage.

At least it was clear that she was not proud of her behavior.

He stepped into the chaise behind the two women and took his seat across from them. He pounded a fist on the wall of the chaise, which pulled forward slowly, navigating the small space between it and the curricle ahead.

An uncomfortable silence reigned, with Jacques staring through the small window and Miss Cosgrove looking down at her hands in her lap.

"Thank you, Lord Moulinet," said Lady Caroline. There was no embarrassment in her tone, only genuine gratitude.

Jacques closed his eyes to muster patience and nodded, not trusting himself to say anything more. Lady Caroline's affairs were hardly any of his business. She seemed to care very little about her reputation or the reactions elicited by her behavior. Indeed, from what Jacques had heard, she almost seemed to *seek out* attention, whether it be good or bad.

Lady Caroline watched him for a moment before resting her head against the seat and maintaining silence. Perhaps she had understood that Jacques had no desire to discuss what had just happened.

Jacques dabbed his handkerchief at his nose and the corner of his eye, which were both still bleeding slightly. What kind of story would he be obliged to concoct to account for his injuries?

"I hope," he finally said as they entered the streets of London, "that it will not inconvenience you, Lady Caroline, if we convey Miss Cosgrove to her home first. I think we must try to avoid any hint of damage to her reputation—even if she *is* dressed as a gentleman—and your presence here is necessary to ensure that. I will then take a hackney and follow you to ensure your safe arrival in Grosvenor Square."

"Of course," Lady Caroline said, nodding swiftly. "But I assure you that your escort to my home is unnecessary. I am very used to being driven around town alone."

Jacques's eyebrows went up. "At this hour of night?"

Her only response was a smile.

He thought of the rumors he had heard—ones which had been

impossible to ignore for how frequently they came up in conversation —about Lord Byron and her. She seemed to have not a shred of regard for scandal.

"Be that as it may," he said, "I would feel more at ease if I could ensure your safety.

"You already have," she said, indicating his hand, of which the knuckles were raw and puffy.

"All the more reason to see that my efforts aren't for naught."

She only nodded in response.

The chaise slowed, and Miss Cosgrove's head came up to look out of the window.

Jacques raised himself from the chaise seat, wincing—his muscles were already taut and achy.

Out of habit, he exited the chaise and moved to put out a hand for Miss Cosgrove. But when her tentative head emerged, topped with a beaver hat, and her foot encased in tall black boots, he withdrew his hand. If anyone were watching, it would appear highly unusual for one healthy young man to assist another healthy young man down from a chaise.

He felt his anger flare up again. It was no thanks to her foolish decisions that she *was* healthy. What if he had not been at the prize fight? She could have been hurt, discovered, or... He exhaled sharply. It didn't bear considering.

"Lord Moulinet?" Lady Caroline said.

Miss Cosgrove turned around as well, but receiving a gesture from Lady Caroline to continue on, she started toward the house, her head turning from side to side, scanning the empty street nervously.

Jacques raised his brows in a question at Lady Caroline.

"My lord," said Lady Caroline, glancing at Miss Cosgrove, "you must be terribly angry. But please spare Cecilia. It was my idea, not hers." She held his gaze for a moment and then nodded and ducked back into the chaise.

Jacques grimaced and then strode quickly to Miss Cosgrove, who was coming up on the front door.

He watched her shoulders come up, as though she were inhaling deeply. She turned toward him, meeting his eyes for the first time. Her gaze moved to the injuries on his face, and she winced. He imagined that the brighter lights of the London streets made his wounds all the more visible and harsh.

"May I attend to those for you, my lord?" she said.

He shook his head, wishing he could say, "*There would be nothing to attend to if not for your foolhardiness.*"

But he settled for, "The Broussard servants are more than capable of assisting me when I arrive there."

Miss Cosgrove's eyes widened a moment in panic, and Jacques felt a rush of irritation. *Now* she was worried about the talk her behavior might occasion?"

"Don't worry," he said, managing to smother the acid tone which the words begged him to assume, "I will not betray you."

She swallowed and nodded, averting her eyes. "I am terribly sorry," she said, one of her hands resting on the iron railing. "I never thought..." she trailed off.

"Yes," Jacques said, "that much is quite clear."

Her eyes jumped to his, and he saw the hurt in them.

How had anyone been deceived by her disguise? She looked every bit a woman, even in buckskin pantaloons and a brown waistcoat.

Her shoulders came up in a helpless gesture. "I merely wanted," she said, "to be someone else for once—free of expectation or recognition." She shut her eyes and shook her head. "You cannot possibly understand what it is like to be valued for one thing only—something you have no control over."

He felt a bit of his anger melting away. "I understand more than you know."

She looked at him doubtfully and then said. "It was one night—one night where I could forget who everyone wants and insists that I be."

Jacques grimaced and shook his head. "Don't you see? Tonight you only traded one mask for another."

Her shimmering eyes held his, and he felt his anger ebb and an impulse to take her hand and comfort her—and then berate her at length for putting herself in harm's way.

"The most important thing," he said, reminding himself as much as her, "is that you are safe. Allow me to call on you tomorrow with Letty. She has been missing you terribly."

Miss Cosgrove laughed weakly. "I saw her not three days ago."

"Ah," said Jacques with a half-smile, "but that is an eternity to Letty." He bowed to her and turned back toward the chaise.

When Jacques entered the morning room to inform Letty that the curricle awaited them outside, she cried out at the sight of him.

"Good heavens, Jacques! Whatever has happened to you!"

Jacques smiled and put out a hand to help her up from the chaise she sat on, perusing the latest edition of *La Belle Assemblée.* "That must be the most unhandsome greeting I have ever received. I think I look quite well today, for your information."

Her eyes widened even more as she came to a stand and had a closer view of the injuries. Jacques was only glad that she had not been there to see them the night before.

The servants had done a fine job of minimizing the damage, though, with the use of poultices and creams.

"Really, Jacques, what on earth happened? I saw you at dinner last night, and your face was perfectly handsome."

Jacques threw his head back in a laugh. "You become more offensive by the minute, Letty. I assure you that I am quite all right. But Miss Cosgrove is waiting for us, so let us not make her wait any longer."

Letty pursed her lips and furrowed her brow as if she would persist, but she followed Jacques out to the curricle.

When Miss Cosgrove entered the morning room in Belport Street, she looked calm and collected—a contrast from her remorseful and anxious demeanor the night before.

Letty greeted her with an energetic embrace, and Jacques bowed with a smile he hoped was free of any reserve.

"Wait a moment," Letty said, looking back and forth between Jacques and Miss Cosgrove with suspicion. "You do not seem at all surprised by Jacques's face which, as far as I can tell, has been mauled by some creature or other!"

"Good gracious, Letty," said Jacques. "Have done with the insults! Perhaps Miss Cosgrove simply possesses a mind of higher caliber than yours—one less preoccupied with appearances." He shot Letty a significant and chastising look.

She laughed aloud. "Cecy?" She waved a hand. "No one could be *more* preoccupied with appearances!"

Jacques watched Miss Cosgrove, who attempted a laugh.

Letty seemed to realize that her words had caused offense rather than amusement, and she walked over to Miss Cosgrove. "Oh dear, I have said something unkind, haven't I? Oh, forgive me, Cecy! You know I didn't mean it that way."

Miss Cosgrove patted Letty's hand. "You have spoken truth, Letty. Only it is a failing that I am working to rid myself of. That is all." She smiled and winked at Letty, who watched her through narrowed eyes, as if she didn't know whether to believe her cousin's nonchalance.

A servant set down a tray of biscuits on the nearest table, and Letty took one from the platter. "I suppose I must believe you, but I hope you will believe that I am very sorry for my wicked words, and that there is no one I love more than you!" She took a bite from the biscuit. "In any case, you *must* absolutely help me solve the mystery of Jacques's injuries, for he seems intent on keeping all the most exciting secrets from me."

Jacques sent an apologetic glance at Miss Cosgrove, whose conscience-stricken expression had reappeared, then smiled at Letty teasingly.

"You are powerless to wrest my secrets—"

"It is my fault," Miss Cosgrove said.

Jacques's mouth hung open, a biscuit at his lips, and he stared at her. Letty, too, looked at Miss Cosgrove with confusion.

"Whatever do you mean?" Letty said with an uncertain laugh.

"It was my folly that caused his injury," she said simply.

Letty looked back and forth between them and reared back slightly. "Well, you must positively not leave me to guess what you mean, Cecy! How in the world should you be responsible for Jacques's face looking like a bruised tomato?"

Jacques sent her a look of feigned offense and then said, "Miss Cosgrove, there is no need at all for you to—"

"I allowed," Miss Cosgrove said determinedly, "myself to be convinced to accompany Lady Caroline to a prize fight."

Letty's eyes bulged, and her jaw hung agape. Finally she said, "And Jacques was in the match?"

Miss Cosgrove tilted her head from side to side. "Not exactly. At least not at first. It was Lady Caroline's idea that we attend dressed as gentlemen, so I borrowed Tobias's clothing, and we were quite unknown"— she cast a hesitant glance at Jacques —"until we saw Lord Retsford, and, knowing how I dislike him, Lady Caroline decided to teach him a lesson."

Jacques looked to Letty, whose eyes were alight with excitement and awe.

"Teach him what kind of lesson?" she said.

Miss Cosgrove sent another darting glance at Jacques. "Well, she wished for me to tell him exactly what I thought of him—"

Letty gasped. "Surely you didn't!"

"I surely did *not*," returned Miss Cosgrove, "for I am not so very lost to reason as to suppose that such a thing could have ended well. We settled instead for walking past him, and Lady Caroline bumped into him as we did so—purposefully, I believe." She took in a large breath and sighed. "One thing led to another, and the crowd began chanting for the marquess and Lady Caroline to engage in their own fight. the marquess was only too happy to oblige."

Letty's hand flew to her mouth. Her eyes shifted to Jacques, and her hand came down slowly. "And you saved them by fighting him yourself," she said in an awed voice.

"He did."

Jacques scoffed, feeling uncomfortable at the way Letty seemed to be enjoying the tale—and the role she had apparently cast him in.

Letty's head shook from side to side slowly as she stared wide-eyed at Jacques, clasping her hands together. "How very romantic."

A slight blush stole into Miss Cosgrove's cheeks, and she avoided Jacques's eye.

Did it embarrass Miss Cosgrove to think that there might have been something more to his actions than mere chivalry?

"I imagine," Miss Cosgrove said, "that romantics were very near the last thing on Lord Moulinet's mind as he was struck again and again by the marquess."

Jacques reared back. "You make it sound as though I were constantly assaulted by the marquess, with never a blow returned."

Letty's head whipped around to him. "Were you knocked unconscious? Did Cecy have to...*revive* you?"

Jacques let out an impatient noise, his own neck and face heating up. "I must clearly speak to your mother about your consumption of romantic novels, Letty! I was decidedly *not* knocked unconscious."

"No," said Miss Cosgrove simply with a small smile, "the shoe was rather on the other foot, in fact."

Jacques wondered if it was possible for Letty's eyes to open any wider without causing her injury.

"You won?" she said.

Jacques nodded, trying to suppress a laugh. "And your surprise is yet another example of the sure protection you provide against my ever developing an overinflated opinion of myself."

"Well," Letty said significantly, "I am *very* sorry to have missed all of the adventure. And I think it is terribly selfish of the two of you to have kept it all to yourselves."

Jacques and Miss Cosgrove exchanged meaningful glances.

"It was *not* an adventure, Letty," said Miss Cosgrove severely, "but a piece of folly which could very easily have ended in a complete loss of my reputation." She paused a moment, and a smile trembled at the corner of her mouth. "Though I must say that it was very satisfying to see someone teach the marquess a lesson, and part of me wishes that he knew I was there to witness his defeat."

Jacques smiled responsively. He sympathized with her sentiment. It had been satisfying to him, too.

"But alas," she said with a discontented sigh, "I am afraid I shall have to continue being civil to him."

"And Lady Caroline the initiator of all this adventure..." Letty said dazedly. "She is a wonder, isn't she?"

Jacques frowned. "Lady Caroline is a very amiable woman, Letty, but hers is not an example I would ever wish you to follow."

"Ever?" said Miss Cosgrove, taken aback. "You are too harsh, surely."

Jacques shook his head. "She cares not a shred for what anyone thinks of her behavior, and it leads her to indiscretion after indiscretion."

"Perhaps," said Miss Cosgrove, her chin up, "but that is what is so wonderful about her—that she is entirely unconcerned with what society says or thinks of her. Besides, I thought you despised those who conformed too strictly to society's expectations."

Letty nodded, looking to Jacques for an explanation.

"It is more than that," he said grimly. "Lady Caroline takes pains to flout society. It may look like freedom, but it is actually a veiled overconcern with society's expectations—an obsession that drives and determines the decisions she makes, based off what will shock and scandalize. *That* is not freedom."

Letty and Miss Cosgrove were both silent, and Jacques hoped that his point had been taken.

"Lady Caroline escapes the majority of undesirable consequences," he continued, "because of the protection her title and connections afford. If anyone of less influence than her tried to attempt what she does"— he grimaced and shook his head —"they would be cut and ostracized."

His argument met no resistance, and he breathed an inward sigh of relief. The last thing he needed was for Letty to follow in Lady Caroline's footsteps—or to be obliged to rescue Miss Cosgrove from doing so again.

⁂

Jacques picked up his pace as he walked Bond Street. The pantaloons he had worn to the prize fight had been stained past saving by a mixture of blood, sweat, and dirt, so he had spent the morning commissioning a handful of pieces of clothing. What good was coming to London if one didn't take full advantage of the skilled tailors there?

His wounds were healing more quickly than he had anticipated— a fact for which he was grateful, as he found it very uncomfortable to satisfy people's questions about their origin.

He had sworn Letty to secrecy about what Miss Cosgrove had revealed concerning the impromptu match between him and Lord Retsford, and he hoped that she would be wise enough to keep her vow of silence.

He was brought up short by a standing figure blocking his way.

"Ah," said the man, "Lord Moulinet."

Jacques looked up to see the sneering half-smile of the marquess, whose face still contained bruising and swelling from their encounter at Harford. Jacques stifled a resigned sigh and nodded his greeting.

"My congratulations on your victory the other night," said the marquess. "You caught me on an evening when I was not at my best."

Jacques inclined his head. "I am sorry if you felt that the circumstances of the fight were unfair, my lord. I bid you good day." He moved to walk around the marquess, but the man moved to prevent him.

"Forgive me," said Lord Retsford, "but there is something very familiar about you that I cannot for the life of me seem to place." He smiled humorlessly at Jacques, who frowned.

"Fear not, though," continued the marquess, "I am determined to solve the mystery. '*Something is rotten in the state of Denmark,*' I think."

Jacques swallowed and clenched his jaw, forcing a smile. "Perhaps the stench is not coming from me, my lord." He nodded again and took a wide step to the side, allowing him to pass by the marquess undeterred.

He felt his heart beating rapidly. Whether the marquess had indeed pegged Jacques for an impostor or whether he was simply determined to do his reputation harm, the fact remained: Jacques had secrets which, if ferreted out, would be his ruin.

His only consolation: no one among the society they kept knew of his charade.

❧ 13 ❧

Cecilia scanned the room full of dominos, noting how her vision seemed constricted by the slits of her eye mask, creating a black frame around her line of sight.

It was Letty's first time to a masquerade, and her buzzing excitement had brought an appreciative smile to Cecilia's face. Her wide-eyed admiration of Ranelagh Gardens had induced a wave of nostalgia in Cecilia for the time when she had felt awe and thrill at such sights. It was only months behind her and yet seemed distant.

Letty was unrecognizable under her silver mask, which covered her entire face, while Cecilia had chosen to wear the same costume she had worn at the last masquerade she had attended: an Egyptian half-mask with gold braiding around the edges and black braiding around the eye slits. She had no desire to be completely anonymous. After the incident at the Harford prize fight, the thought of anonymity left a bad taste in her mouth.

Lord Moulinet wore a dark blue domino and a half-mask, and Cecilia stared at how bright and fierce looked the eye on the uncovered side of his face. Mrs. Broussard had adopted an Elizabethan costume with an exceptionally tall neck ruff and wrist ruffs to match.

Letty let out a disgusted noise, and Cecilia glanced at her with a frown. "What is it?"

"Him," Letty replied, indicating with her head a man nearby in a knight costume. The visor was raised so that there was no mistaking his identity: the marquess of Retsford.

Cecilia sighed. "I can only imagine it will be quite awful to dance with him in that clanking, bulky costume."

"I am more than willing," said Lord Moulinet, "to do what I can to spare you that necessity. Would you care to dance with me instead?"

Cecilia smiled gratefully and placed her hand on the arm he extended to her. Was there anyone in the room she would prefer to dance with more than Lord Moulinet? She couldn't think of a single gentleman. And that was in spite of the residual shame and contrition she felt which made Lord Moulinet's company less comfortable than usual. She hated knowing that he disapproved of her behavior.

But his behavior toward her held no reserve or disapprobation as they took their place among the set.

"How are your wounds, my lord?" she said as they joined hands to move down the set.

"Nearly healed, thank you," he said amiably.

They took their places across from one another again. "I am very sorry to have been the cause of such a terrible ordeal for you."

He shook his head. "What is past is done. I am glad that I was there to prevent you from coming to harm. I hope you know that my anger was merely fear for what might have occurred had I not made the decision—a very uncharacteristic one, mind you"— he smiled at her, and she felt tingling in her skin —"to attend."

"But you needn't have intervened. You had no obligation to do so. Why not simply let us experience the consequences of our decisions?"

He blew a laugh through his nose, even as his brows furrowed. "What a fellow you must think me. I could never leave someone I care about to such a fate."

Cecilia swallowed. Of course he meant nothing by the phrase *someone I care about.*

"Well, I am forever indebted to you for it. I am afraid it cannot have done anything to abate the marquess's dislike of you, though."

The vicomte chuckled. "No, certainly not. He is no admirer of mine. I believe he has made it a personal goal to embarrass me in whatever way he possibly can."

"Hmph," Cecilia said incredulously. "And how should he accomplish such a thing? In at least one way you proved yourself his superior. And I hardly think any woman in this room would debate which of you two is more handsome or charming or amiable—or younger, for that matter."

Lord Moulinet's ears turned red, and Cecilia realized, with a blush of her own, how forward her comment had been.

"Letty would certainly not agree with you," he said with a wry smile.

Cecilia laughed, her eyes searching out her cousin. She was not, as Cecilia had anticipated, standing next to Aunt Emily, but was shoulder to shoulder with a young woman in a purple domino and matching mask. Cecilia's mouth twisted to the side. Where *was* Aunt Emily?

"You dislike Lady Caroline's example for Letty," said Cecilia, "but what say you to the influence of someone like Priscilla Fletcher?"

Lord Moulinet turned his head to look for Letty. He grimaced when he saw who she stood with. "Where is Aunt Emily?"

Cecilia shrugged. "I wouldn't put it past Priscilla to have concocted some plan to distract her. She is always up to some mischief or other."

"Happily," said the vicomte with a light smile, "she is not our concern."

The dance took them apart for a time, and Cecilia couldn't help but glance again to where Letty had been standing when they came together again. Priscilla Fletcher stood in the same spot, her mother standing at her side. Aunt Emily stood not far off, her head leaning in toward the woman next to her as though they wished to be private.

Letty was nowhere to be seen.

"She is gone," Cecilia said, her eyes searching all over for the silver domino and mask as Lord Moulinet joined her.

They broke apart as the last note of the song was played, and Cecilia made a swift curtsy, matched by the perfunctory bow of Lord Moulinet. There was one more song in the set, but as she met eyes with Lord Moulinet, he said, "Perhaps we should..."

Cecilia nodded.

The vicomte escorted her off of the ballroom floor, and they headed toward Aunt Emily but came upon Mary Holledge first.

"Mary," said Cecilia, slightly breathless, "have you seen Letty anywhere?"

Mary shook her head. "No, I haven't seen her all evening."

Cecilia's brow wrinkled. "She is wearing a full mask, so I suppose it is no wonder you didn't recognize her."

"Wait," Mary said, her eyes narrowing as she rested a hand on Cecilia's arm. "A full mask and a silver domino?"

Cecilia nodded, swallowing.

Mary clenched her teeth, pointing toward the tall, white French doors. "I saw her walk out onto the terrace with Lord Retsford—though if I had known it was her, I should have tried to stop her."

"Thank you," Cecilia said quickly, as Lord Moulinet rushed away toward the large doors which opened onto the terrace and into the gardens.

She followed behind him, her heart beating erratically. Why would Letty do something so foolish with a man she held in aversion?

Lord Moulinet squeezed past a pair of ladies walking through the doors and out onto the walled terrace. Cecilia joined him, looking over the rows of perfectly-aligned trees, the long encased pond, and the elaborate *maison chinoise* that seemed to float in the middle.

"There," Cecilia said, seeing the conspicuous silver armor of the marquess. "In the Chinese House."

They rushed down the steps, brushing past the couples walking leisurely along the tree-lined path. Lord Moulinet's eyes were fixed on his cousin and the marquess, who stood opposite one another, the marquess resting an elbow on the stone wall, Letty with her hands clasped behind her back, her mask off entirely.

What in the world were they doing?

"Letty," Lord Moulinet said breathlessly, a hint of censure in his voice as they came upon them.

"Ah," said Lord Retsford, not even rising from his reclined posture as Cecilia and the vicomte stepped up into the *maison*. "The man himself, no doubt come to rescue you from my wiles. And joined by his greatest admirer, I see." He smiled at Cecilia with a hint of a sneer tugging at the corner of his mouth.

"Letty," said Cecilia, pointedly ignoring the marquess, "I think we should return to the rotunda." She put out a hand, and Letty nodded, her eyes overbright.

The vicomte turned to follow them, and the marquess's voice carried behind them. "I was just learning," he said, "about some of your fascinating history, Lord Moulinet."

Why did he say the vicomte's name with such a mocking tone?

The vicomte barely turned around, inclining his head politely and saying, "I am glad if it entertained you. Good evening, my lord." He turned and kept walking.

"What in the world were you thinking, Letty?" Cecilia said. "To be seen roaming the gardens with Lord Retsford is enough to ruin your reputation."

"Not when no one knows who I am," said Letty defensively. "Besides, that is very rich coming from the woman who disappeared with him at the Ferguson's rout."

Cecilia's mouth opened and closed wordlessly. She could hardly refute the charge laid against her, but she had to force herself not to look at the vicomte for his reaction to the words. He seemed to have more and more reason to think ill of her with each thing he discovered.

But how had Letty even known? It had been before her arrival in town, at a time when Cecilia had felt intoxicated by the victory of having the marquess's attentions directed toward her.

As if reading Cecilia's thoughts, Letty turned around, stopping on the terrace. "Priscilla told me," she said simply.

"I suppose I should have guessed that," Cecilia said with a grimace. "It was a naïve piece of idiocy—the very type I have been trying to warn you against. I hope you can learn from *my* mistakes instead of insisting on making them yourself."

Letty pouted slightly. "All I was trying to do was help you."

Cecilia met Lord Moulinet's gaze, both looking incredulous.

"Forgive me," said the vicomte, "but I can't say that I see how escaping outside with the marquess is helping Miss Cosgrove."

Letty crossed her arms defensively, her mask still in her hand, and looked at him through narrowed eyes before turning to Cecilia with a mischievous smile twitching at the corner of her lip. "You said you wished you could tell Lord Retsford just what you thought of him. Well"— she shrugged her shoulders —"I thought I might do it *for* you since I am perfectly anonymous in this costume." She raised the mask to her face, and Cecilia could imagine her smiling behind it.

"Good heavens," said Cecilia, dismayed. Her eyes darted to Lord Moulinet, who closed his eyes and shook his head in a patience-summoning gesture. "What an idea, Letty! I hope you thought better of it."

"I am not such a coward!" Letty said, letting the mask drop from her face. "*But* I let him flirt with me for a few minutes before delivering my speech"— she smiled at the thought, staring out into the gardens as if remembering a sweet victory —"so that he might be even more embarrassed than ever when I ripped his character to shreds." She turned back toward them. "It was Priscilla's idea."

"Letty, Letty, Letty," said the vicomte. "Do you have any original ideas, or do they all originate with Priscilla Fletcher?" He took the mask from her hand and waved it in front of her face. "Besides, your costume only offers you anonymity when you *wear* it. And you were decidedly *sans masque* when we came upon you."

"Yes, well," said Letty, lifting her chin as her mouth returned to a pout, "it wasn't until after I had delivered my speech that the marquess made it clear that he already knew my identity."

Cecilia swallowed.

"Even had he not known," said Lord Moulinet, "he could easily have asked around after the fact. It would not be difficult to discover your identity."

"Was he angry?" Cecilia said, imagining with misgiving what someone as arrogant as the marquess would do after being so blatantly insulted.

Letty shook her head rapidly. "No, he was only amused." She frowned. "In fact, he was mostly interested in talking about *you*"— she indicated the vicomte —"asking me question after question."

Cecilia's brows knit, and she looked at Lord Moulinet, who shot her a quick, humorless smile. "He is determined to discover something—anything—unsavory about my character and my past."

Cecilia scoffed. "So he assumes that everyone is as reprehensible as himself?"

Lord Moulinet looked at her in a way that made her heart flutter.

How he was still able to countenance her company was something she struggled to understand, after all she had done to give him a distaste for it. But she was certainly grateful that he seemed not to dislike spending time with her.

When they were back inside the rotunda and had conveyed Letty back to the safety of her mother's chaperonage, Cecilia turned to the vicomte and took in a large breath. It was never easy to admit wrong.

"I find myself in a semi-constant state of needing to apologize to you," she said with a humorous grimace. "It is very vexing."

He smiled widely but tilted his head as if he was unsure what she meant.

"It was *my* words," she said, "that inspired Letty this evening. Surely when I spoke of my desire to tell him what I thought of him…"

He shook his head and waved his hand dismissively. "You could never have known that she would take your words as an invitation to act. Besides, I distinctly remember you saying that you weren't foolish enough to think such an endeavor would end well."

Cecilia swallowed uncomfortably, hesitant to draw his attention to more of her foolish behavior. "But in combination with the example she feels I have set for her..." her voice trailed off, and she averted her eyes.

Why was it so hard to pretend confidence in his company? And why did she feel she had to be perfectly clear with him about her failings? Two months ago, she would have done nearly anything to avoid admitting such things.

"Miss Cosgrove," said the vicomte in an amused voice, "if you believe yourself to be the only person to have ever made unwise decisions, let me disabuse you of such a notion at once."

She looked up at him tentatively, feeling a glimmer of hope. "*You* at least seem to be free of such failings."

He shook his head. "Far from it."

She couldn't help it. She wanted to know more about this man who was still so mysterious to her in many ways. She tilted her head and looked at him with doubtful, teasing eyes. "I don't know if I believe you. Though I suppose," she said in a cryptic voice, "you might have a very sordid past that all of us are completely ignorant of." Her smile wavered as she looked at him.

He forced a smile and a breathy chuckle.

She blinked rapidly. What had she said?

He excused himself with a bow and a more convincing smile under the guise of having promised a dance to someone.

A prickle of jealousy flared up inside, and Cecilia only nodded stiffly, looking after his retreating figure with a sense of loneliness.

What, did she expect him to dance attendance upon her and only her all evening long? She was becoming almost as silly as Letty.

She turned away determinedly.

She needed to get her emotions under control quickly.

14

Jacques sat down to breakfast the day after the masquerade with a crease in his brow. He had been fighting off ill-humor ever since Miss Cosgrove's comment about his sordid past.

Little did she know how near the mark she had hit.

But to her, such a possibility was laughable—and only *because* it was unbelievable.

It was with dismay that she had seen his reaction to her joke. And he had known a moment of wishing to tell her everything.

She had become so open and genuine with him that he wished—painfully wished—that he could do the same.

But he couldn't. And he hated that he couldn't. He hated deceiving her into thinking that he was something so far from what he truly was.

He stared at the food on his plate for a moment, then scooted his chair back and strode out of the room.

He needed to speak with his father. Whether Jacques wanted to reveal his past or not, the marquess was certainly determined to ferret out damaging information about him. Jacques doubted he could manage such a feat—it had been more than twenty years since their arrival, after all—but he needed to be sure that there was no way the man could discover their ruse.

He knocked lightly on his father's bedroom door and opened it when he heard his father's voice welcome him in.

His father's valet stood behind him, making a few final touches to the small curls gathered in a band behind the Comte's head. He wore an elaborate silk dressing gown—he had always been much more comfortable flaunting himself in expensive clothing than Jacques. Sometimes Jacques thought his father truly *was* made to be a Comte.

"Oh," his father said with a smile, turning around so that his valet's nostrils flared in annoyance. "I hadn't expected *you*, Jacques."

Jacques smiled perfunctorily. "I thought I would pay you a visit since the rest of the world has been up for hours, and you haven't yet made an appearance."

His father laughed jovially and slapped him on the shoulder. "When you're my age, you'll do the same, *mon fils*."

Jacques smiled and glanced at the valet. Following his gaze, his father looked at the valet and back to Jacques before saying, "*Merci, Fortin.*" The valet executed a deep bow and left them to themselves.

"What is it, Jacques?" his father said as he sat on the edge of the bed. "I assume that you wish to be private with me, or else you would have simply waited for me to come down to breakfast."

Jacques nodded and inhaled. "Father, is there anyone who might be aware of our true identities?"

His father began shaking his head, but Jacques pressed on. "Anyone at all, Father. A servant who assisted the Comte upon arrival in Dover, even?"

His father shook his head again. "I sent one of the shipmen ahead of us to the inn to ensure that a room should be prepared for the Comte to rest in. When we arrived at the inn, we went straight to the room."

Jacques worried his lip. "So the shipman you sent *would* be aware that you are not the true Comte de Montreuil?"

His father scoffed. "A French shipman twenty years ago who

returned immediately to France and likely never gave us a second thought?" He looked at Jacques curiously. "Why are you asking me this? We have discussed this before."

Jacques grimaced and shook his head. Surely he was just being ridiculous. The marquess would hardly be able to search out a solitary Frenchman who worked on the packet twenty years ago—and even if he managed such a feat, the likelihood of the man remembering such a commonplace event was so unlikely as to be absurd.

"Nothing," he said with a small laugh at himself. "You know how I am prone to worry."

His father squeezed his shoulder. "None better, I should think." He stood. "Come breakfast with me. I am feeling very sociable today and may even venture out with you this evening to whatever gathering you plan on attending." He wagged his eyebrows. Having little interest in the balls and parties that Jacques found himself attending, his father had been accompanying Mr. Broussard to his club.

In fact, Jacques was surprised at his own level of social involvement since his arrival in town. He had not anticipated that he would be engaged every evening of the week, and he had a sneaking suspicion that the underlying motivator for his unwonted levels of social engagement had much to do with Miss Cosgrove.

Of course, she was often frustratingly proud and maddeningly foolish, but there was also an ever-growing streak of vulnerability and kindness that had been entirely unexpected after their first interaction. His first judgments of her had been uncharitable. Knowing more about her background and experiences, he found himself sympathizing with her more often than not—even when he wished to shake her and remind her that a gentleman worth his salt would prefer the unaffected, kind woman behind the mask she sometimes donned.

Thankfully, she seemed to be spending more and more time without the mask. And the more time she spent without the mask, the more time Jacques found himself wishing to spend with her.

What a mess he was entangling himself in.

I t was with a flicker of joy that Jacques caught sight of Miss Cosgrove that evening. Gone was much of the rigidity with which she had carried herself a few weeks ago, and the enjoyment on her face was more genuine than it was arch or calculated. It pleased Jacques greatly to see.

If his joy was dampened slightly upon realizing that she was so cheerfully engaged in a country dance with another gentleman, Jacques didn't allow himself to dwell on the silly spark of jealousy for more than a moment.

His father stood next to him, looking more like a Macaroni than Jacques could have wished, but nothing could dampen his father's confidence, no matter how often Jacques suggested that he dress with less pomp and pageantry.

The set ended on the ballroom floor, and Jacques noted with a little self-deprecating chuckle how he instinctively stood straighter as he watched Miss Cosgrove's partner escort her back to her mother.

"Come, Father," he said, his eyes still on her. "I don't believe you have yet had the opportunity to meet the Cosgroves."

His father followed him over to where Mrs. Cosgrove and her daughter stood, joined predictably by Letty and her mother.

Miss Cosgrove looked at him with a smile that turned curious upon seeing his father.

Jacques introduced the two Cosgrove women to his father, noting the obvious, admiring light with which he regarded Miss Cosgrove.

"Well," said his father, making a flourishing bow to the women, "I thought I had seen all the most beautiful sights London had to offer, but I see that I was terribly wrong."

Jacques's jaw tightened, and he looked an apology at Miss Cosgrove when her eyes darted to him, unsure what to make of his father. Here he had chastised Miss Cosgrove for making too much of her appearance, only to have his own father call attention to it before she had ever said a word.

Miss Cosgrove smiled politely and curtsied. "You betray your ignorance of London, my lord, by saying such things. Perhaps your son can better acquaint you with the spectacular sights the town has to offer."

Jacque's father looked at him with incredulity. "I find myself at a loss to understand my own son. With such a charming woman in front of you, what precisely are you waiting for?"

"Why, Uncle," Letty cried. "That's a famous idea! I can hardly imagine anything better than a marriage between my two dearest cousins!"

Miss Cosgrove's eyebrows went up, and her cheeks flushed, reflecting the color Jacques was tolerably sure his own face had turned. He cleared his throat. "I think my father was referring to the set that is forming, Letty."

His father scoffed. "Think again, *mon fils.*"

Ignoring the continuing humiliating nature of his father's comments, Jacques offered his arm to Miss Cosgrove, intent upon apologizing profusely for his father's lack of tact.

When they were far enough out of range that their conversation wouldn't be heard, though, Miss Cosgrove was the first to speak.

"I confess that your father is nothing like I had imagined he would be."

"What, completely lacking in social graces and dressed as though time stopped fifty years ago?"

She laughed aloud. "You are unkind. I suppose I should have expected that the person who raised *you* would be completely lacking affectation."

He looked at her reflectively. "I am sorry that he fixated upon your appearance. The irony was not lost upon me, having censured you in the past for placing too much importance upon such things."

She shrugged. "I am too accustomed to it to take offense. Indeed, his words would have pleased me considerably even a month ago." She sighed dramatically. "But, alas, I have spent enough time in your company that my arrogance has been reduced to a shadow of what it once was." She stole a teasing glance at him, and it made his mouth feel suddenly dry.

"Would you like to forego this dance in favor of some refreshment?" He watched as her smile faded slightly, a more intent look in her eyes.

She nodded. "I should like it very much."

With two glasses of ratafia in hand, they made their way to the nearest seats.

"You and your father escaped from France together, then?" she asked, thanking him as he handed her down into the seat.

Jacques felt his muscles tense slightly, just as they did anytime the past was brought up. "Yes," he said. "My mother died in childbirth, so it was only ever the two of us."

Her features softened, and her head shook slightly. "I am so sorry."

He offered something between a smile and a grimace. "I am sorry, too, that I was never able to meet her. I have heard plenty of stories from my father, of course, but"— he raised his brows and tilted his head —"as you have witnessed for yourself, my father is prone to exaggeration."

Miss Cosgrove shifted her knees toward him and blinked slowly in an expression of feigned offense. "You mean to say that his comments on my beauty were simple exaggeration?"

"That is not what I meant."

"Pray, what *did* you mean, then?"

It was evident from the way her mouth quivered that Miss Cosgrove was thoroughly enjoying his discomfiture.

"I meant," he said slowly, realizing that there was hardly a satisfactory explanation for his comment, "that you might have noticed how his *general manner* tends toward excess and overstatement."

She smoothed her dress with a hand in an overly formal gesture. "I thought his choice of clothing very..."

Jacques's mouth twitched as she struggled for words.

"...very..."

"Ancestral?" he offered, his shoulders shaking.

She took her lips between her teeth to stop a laugh. "Precisely."

They met eyes, and he imagined that his own carried the same twinkle as hers, his smile the same joyful shape as her soft, pink lips.

Their time together seemed to end so quickly that Jacques wondered if the orchestra had not selected the briefest songs in their repertoire on purpose—to defy his desire to remain with Miss Cosgrove as long as possible. He tried not to betray his reluctance to convey her back to her mother, but he could have sworn that she, too, looked surprised when the strings strung out their last note.

No sooner was she at her mother's side than she was approached by yet another gentleman wishing for his chance at some privacy with her. Jacques suppressed a resigned sigh, coming to stand next to his father again.

"She's the one, Jacques," his father said, continuing his apathetic scanning of the room.

Jacques let out a scoffing noise. "Thank you, Father. You already made it quite clear to me—*and* to Miss Cosgrove *and* Aunt Emily *and* Letty—that those were your feelings."

His father took a glass of wine from the passing footman. "Don't be a fool, then, Jacques. And don't, for heaven's sake, try to pretend that you aren't giddy over the girl. I was watching the two of you, and a pair of young people more mad after one another you would be hard-pressed to find."

The eruption of hope he felt upon hearing his father's words Jacques set determinedly aside. "If you were in my position," he said, watching Miss Cosgrove and her partner join hands, "could you inflict the deceit upon her that *I* would be obliged to inflict upon Miss Cosgrove? Assuming that she does care about me in such a way, which is no sure thing."

He watched her say something through a large smile to her partner. Was the smile she offered that man any different than the ones she bestowed upon Jacques? He would be a fool to assume such a thing, particularly when she was being courted by somewhere in the range of a dozen men, including a Marquess.

His father cocked his head to the side. "I don't know," he said. "But I do not think, *mon fils*, that she has fallen in love with your title, and you are the same person with it or without it."

"Try telling that to her father," Jacques said under his breath.

His teeth clenched as he watched the determined approach of Lord Retsford, as if he meant to come offer a reminder of his power and position. His expression was curious as he came to stand before them, his eyes moving again and again to Jacques's father.

"Lord Moulinet," he said with a slight nod. "How very good to happen upon you here. Or I should rather say, happen upon you and..." He looked pointedly at Jacques's father.

Jacques wished he could deny the marquess the introduction he so obviously wished for, but to do so would only pique the man's interest more.

"Lord Retsford," he said with a barely civil smile, "allow me to introduce you to my father, le Comte de Montreuil. Father, this is the Marquess of Retsford."

Lord Retsford was performing his shallow bow, but an arrested expression came into his eyes, which he trained on Jacques's father.

"Yes," he said slowly, "I knew you looked familiar. And I know that name, too. We have met before, have we not?"

Jacques's father shook his head cheerfully, but as he looked at the marquess, his smile flickered slightly and his eyes widened almost imperceptibly—just for a moment.

"No," he said, "I don't believe I have had that pleasure."

"Hmm," said the marquess, "I could have sworn..." He studied the Comte's face again and then straightened. "Well, no matter, it will come to me, I am sure." He looked at Jacques. "I am determined, after all, to become better acquainted with you." He bowed politely with a hint of a sneer at Jacques, and then walked off.

Jacques felt his body relax. "What was *that?*" he asked, turning to his father.

But the color was draining from his father's face. "Jacques," he said slowly, his eyes still staring unblinking at Lord Retsford. "Is that the man who has taken you in dislike?"

Jacques nodded, feeling fear suddenly creep through his veins, coursing toward his heart. "Why? What does it matter?"

His father turned his body slowly away, clenching his eyelids shut. "He was there," he said.

"He was where?"

"At Dover. When we arrived."

Jacques felt himself begin to sweat, a cold sweat that made his gloves cling to the skin on his hands.

"Do you remember?" his father said urgently.

Jacques only shook his head.

"The young man who helped me in the room of the inn with Monsieur le Comte?"

A memory, long since forgotten in the chaos that ensued afterward, struggled to the forefront of Jacques's mind. A man, crouching down next to his father over the Comte's body.

Jacques's eyes bulged, and he looked toward the marquess. There was no mistaking him now. He was much older, yes, but the youthful man was still recognizable underneath.

Jacques swore, tearing his eyes away.

How could his father have told him time and again that there was no one to fear, no one who could *possibly* know of their deception? Not even a servant, he had said only that morning. And all the while, their greatest threat was from a marquess—a marquess determined to ruin Jacques's reputation by any means possible.

Their only hope was that the marquess wouldn't remember the interaction.

What a meager and dim hope it was.

❧ 15 ❧

For what seemed like the fiftieth time that evening, Cecilia quashed an urge to look for the Vicomte de Moulinet. If she was being quite honest with herself, the chance of seeing him and of dancing with him was the only reason she had agreed to come to Lady Heathcote's ball. It was insufferably hot, and the London crowds were beginning to draw thin.

She had a suspicion that the only reason her own family had not made the journey back to Dorset for the more pleasant seaside breeze was due to the continuing presence in town of the marquess—and her father's persistent hope of him asking permission to pay his addresses to Cecilia.

While she in no way shared this hope with her father, she had not dared to bring up the subject of leaving town—not when it would mean the end of her interaction with Lord Moulinet. Nor did she have the courage to tell her father that the marquess's attentions had waned considerably. It seemed that any time he *did* approach her or ask her to dance, it was with an ulterior motive: to get under the vicomte's skin.

But the vicomte was not anywhere to be seen at Lady Heathcote's ball.

Cecilia's heart dropped suddenly. Surely he would not have left town without informing her of the fact?

She scoffed at herself. He owed her no such thing. But she had not been able to quench the hope of his returned regard that had been burgeoning inside her.

She tried to sound disinterested as she said to her mother, "Have you seen Aunt Emily and Letty or the vicomte? I expected them to be here this evening."

"No," her mother said, clearly less troubled by their absence than was Cecilia, "I have not seen them. Nor have I seen Lord Retsford." Her voice held great disappointment, and Cecilia could only be glad that her own relief was unnoticed due to her mother's complete fixation upon surveying the crowd.

It was only moments later that Lady Caroline arrived at the ball, soon making her way to Cecilia's side. She looked thinner and more gaunt than she had at their last meeting—a change which would undoubtedly be attributed by the *ton* to her rejection by Lord Byron.

Cecilia had assumed that Lady Caroline had the best of all worlds, in many ways. Marriage to a man who would inherit a Viscountcy, close connections with Devonshire House and the Prince Regent himself, complete disregard for public opinion, and, added to it all, a determination to follow her heart wherever it led. And it seemed to lead quite determinedly to Lord Byron.

To Cecilia, it appeared a recipe for happiness.

And yet Lady Caroline did not look happy. She flitted from person to person, finally arriving at Cecilia's side where she whispered, only half aware of who she was addressing, "Have you seen him?" Her eyes searched Cecilia's with almost frantic energy.

This was the side of Lady Caroline that inspired more gossip than even her eccentric habit of dressing as a man, and it was Cecilia's first time witnessing it for herself: the mania of her love for Byron.

Cecilia shook her head, troubled at the state of her friend.

Lady Caroline didn't linger after receiving the answer, and Cecilia watched her progress around the room with disturbed awe.

"Mrs. Cosgrove, Miss Cosgrove."

It was the voice of Lord Moulinet, and Cecilia felt her heart leap. He smiled at her, but it was not his usual smile. There was something missing in it; some kind of sadness, perhaps? His eyes regarded her with an evaluative gleam.

What had she done?

"May I accompany Miss Cosgrove to the refreshment table?" he inquired of her mother.

Her mother nodded distractedly, still intently looking for any sign of the Marquess of Retsford. Glad for her mother's preoccupation, Cecilia took Jacques's arm, her regret at having come to Lady Heathcote's ball completely evaporating in his presence.

He led her over to the refreshment table, acquiring some wafers and a drink for them, and then led them over to a bench. There seemed to be a touch of impatience and a rushed feeling to his movements, and it was with misgiving that Cecilia observed him.

"What is it?" she said, accepting a few of the wafers from him.

"I must speak with you," he said, taking a seat beside her as he drew in a deep breath.

"Of course." She smiled, hoping to conceal her nerves.

His lips formed in a tight line, and he looked down at his glass before meeting her eyes again. "From the beginning of our acquaintance, I have censured you for something that I myself am guilty of."

The sound of a raised voice met Cecilia's ears, and she turned her head. Lady Caroline stood a dozen feet away, face to face with Lord Byron. "Oh dear," said Cecilia. "She has found him."

Lord Moulinet looked over with an impatient glance. "Miss Cosgrove," he said, and she turned back toward him.

Lady Caroline was capable of attending to her own affairs. She lowered her drink to her lap and met the vicomte's eyes squarely and attentively.

He smiled wryly, "I think you cannot be unaware of the regard I hold you in. My father informed me that only a fool could be oblivious to it."

Cecilia felt suddenly as though she had forgotten how to breathe properly, and her cheeks warmed as she averted her eyes, not trusting herself to look him in the eye. "I am a fool, then." She glanced up at him, and her breath caught at the warm look in his eyes. "I had hoped," she said, shaking her head, "but I have given you far too many reasons to hold me in disdain that I didn't dare..."

"Disdain?" he said, incredulous. "How could you think such a thing?" His half-smile appeared, and his eyes moved down to her lips. He blinked twice, straightening himself. "But I cannot in good conscience press forward as I should like without being forthright with you about my circumstances"— he held her eyes intently —"about my origins."

Cecilia laughed nervously. "How grave you are. You have me imagining the very worst scenarios."

"What would *be* the worst scenario you could imagine?"

She laughed again, trying to lighten the mood and dispel the gloom he seemed determined to bring to the conversation. "I assure you that my imagination can concoct wilder scenarios than you might suppose—ones that would involve such unlikely stories as you being a wanted Jacobin determined on overthrowing the English monarchy, or a secret spy or"— she sputtered —"some sort of impostor."

He said nothing, only closing his eyes and breathing softly through his nose.

Her smile wavered. "I am only jesting, my lord. I am sure that, whatever you have to tell me, it cannot be so serious as you imagine it to be. The esteem I hold you in"— she swallowed determinedly, wanting to see him smile again and feeling the need to reassure him —"my growing regard is not so flimsy as you seem to think it."

He met her eyes for a moment and then looked away. His brow furrowed as his gaze grew alert. "What in heaven's name?"

Cecilia followed the direction of his gaze, and her eyes bulged.

Lady Caroline stood in front of Lord Byron, wielding a dagger.

She raised her voice and suddenly brought the dagger down, slashing herself in the chest. Cries of shock rang out in the ballroom, and Lord Moulinet shot up from his chair, followed by Cecilia, whose hand flew to her open mouth.

Lady Caroline stood, blood seeping through her clothing, her chest heaving, her face losing color by the second as the onlookers surrounding Lord Byron looked on in paralyzed shock.

Lord Moulinet rushed over to Lady Caroline, gently taking the dagger from her hand and then motioning for Cecilia to assist him.

Cecilia hurried over, her heart racing, and slipped Lady Caroline's arm around her shoulders, trying not to notice the crimson liquid which she could feel seeping through her dress from Lady Caroline's.

There was no resistance from Lady Caroline, who seemed to have lost all energy, and, together with the vicomte, Cecilia supported her across the room and into a corridor, feeling the eyes of dozens of people upon them. They passed by a footman carrying a silver platter, and Lord Moulinet instructed him to call for a doctor without delay.

As they laid Lady Caroline down on a chaise lounge, her lids began to flutter.

"Keep her alert," instructed the vicomte as he walked to the table against the wall, which held the platter of spirits. He set the blood-tinged dagger upon it and picked up one of the decanters. "How does the wound look?"

Cecilia put her hand to Lady Caroline's cheek. "Caro," she said. "Are you all right?"

Lady Caroline's head rocked from side to side, and she mumbled something unintelligible.

Cecilia took in a steadying breath and looked down to the torn bodice of Lady Caroline's dress. The blood on the fabric was a bright crimson, but she could see a gash in the center of the tear where the knife had pierced her skin. "It looks"— Cecilia felt a wave of nausea wash over her and closed her eyes, putting a wrist to her mouth —"It is bleeding, but it does not seem so very deep."

Lord Moulinet came to kneel beside her with a glass of what looked like brandy. "I think this will do you some good," he said, tipping up Lady Caroline's chin, putting the glass to her lips, and pouring some liquid into her mouth.

"What could have possessed her...?" Cecilia said, blinking as she looked at her injured friend. She imagined the mischievous smile of Lady Caroline as they had ventured from their chaise onto the green where the prize fight had taken place. She had always seemed so confident and unruffled. Cecilia had hardly recognized the woman in the ballroom whose outburst they had just witnessed.

Lord Moulinet kept his watchful eyes on Lady Caroline. "People can certainly make some drastic and incomprehensible decisions when they are in love."

Cecilia's eyes flitted to him. Was he only referring to Lady Caroline? Or was this an extension of the conversation they hadn't finished?

The door opened, and a doctor stepped into the room, accompanied by Lady Caroline's husband, whose face was stern, his brow dark and foreboding.

Lord Moulinet and Cecilia both stood, making way for the two men to take their places.

"We will leave you to care for her," said the vicomte with a slight bow. Neither the doctor nor Lady Caroline's husband seemed to pay him any heed, and Cecilia shot a final, worried glance at her friend, who seemed to become more agitated with the arrival of her husband.

They entered the ballroom to the view of covered-mouth whispers and shifting glances. Cecilia's mother approached them, a hand over her bosom.

"There you are," she said with an upward fluttering of her eyes. "Thank heaven! When I heard you had walked off with that woman, I was sure that the next I should hear of you would be that you had been injured by her."

Cecilia reared back, noting Lord Moulinet's frown. "Of course not, Mama. Lady Caroline would never do me an injury."

"If she would do herself an injury," her mother said dismissively, "there is *no one* she wouldn't injure, my dear." She looked down at Cecilia's dress. "Good heavens, you are covered in blood!"

Cecilia glanced down at the blood which had transferred to her dress. "It is of no account," she said.

Mrs. Cosgrove dipped her head, her eyes flitting to the nearby attendees. "I think, Cecilia, that we can agree that you *must* avoid the company of Lady Caroline. We cannot afford to have your reputation damaged by association with someone who commits such abhorrent acts. And in public!"

Cecilia looked an apology at Lord Moulinet, who had stiffened beside her.

"Just think, my dear," her mother continued, "if your chances at marriage were ruined simply from keeping company with a woman as dead to propriety as Lady Caroline."

"Mama," said Cecilia, feeling the heat seep into her cheeks at her mother's uncharitable words, "surely Lady Caroline deserves our sympathy rather than our disdain." Cecilia, too, had been shocked by her friend's conduct and had at first wondered whether perhaps she had made a mistake in getting on such close terms with Lady Caroline.

If it had not been for Lord Moulinet's unhesitating desire to assist Lady Caroline, Cecilia had the uncomfortable suspicion that she might have simply looked on, as everyone else had, in shock and secret condemnation.

"What ideas you have, child," said her mother with a condescending laugh. "How precisely is one to have sympathy for a woman who was the cause of her *own* misfortune and harm? And, again, in public"— she motioned to the room around them —"at a ball of all places!"

"Forgive me, ma'am," said the vicomte with a hint of a bite to his tone, "but does your disapproval of Lady Caroline stem from her behavior or merely from the fact that she failed to keep it private?"

Mrs. Cosgrove blinked twice and stuttered, clearly not expecting to meet argument from the vicomte.

Cecilia's jaw hung open at the uncharacteristic outburst from Lord Moulinet. But his jaw was shifting from side to side, and she could feel his arm muscles tensing beside her.

"Forgive me, ma'am," he said, bowing and excusing himself.

Cecilia nearly called out to him, but she thought better of it. Her mother's company was unlikely to improve his mood, whatever had soured it. Certainly her mother's comments were in poor taste and unfeeling, but the vicomte's reaction seemed unwarranted, given how composed and even-keeled he normally was.

She would have to find another time to discover what was underlying his touchy behavior. And to discover what he had been on the verge of explaining to her before Lady Caroline's episode had interrupted.

"What an angry man the vicomte is," her mother said, watching him walk off with an offended stare. "Come, my dear, we cannot possibly stay here another moment with you looking so morbid."

Cecilia hadn't the energy to resist. Nor did she wish to.

On the carriage ride home, her mother talked almost incessantly, largely focusing on the merits of the marquess as a suitor.

Too drained to try to help her mother see reason, Cecilia laid her head back against the coach seat and found her thoughts making their way, as they so often did, to the vicomte.

With Lady Caroline's injury, Cecilia had not had the opportunity to reflect on or examine the words which she and Lord Moulinet had shared. They had been so wrapped up, too, in the intensity of whatever Lord Moulinet had been on the verge of telling her.

Had she imagined his words? Had she read something into them that he hadn't meant?

"*I think you cannot be unaware of the regard I hold you in,*" he had said.

It was possible that he had not meant anything serious by it—simply the regard of a dear friend.

But she fervently hoped that she had come to mean more than that to him. It felt too fantastic to be true, of course, but Cecilia could no more force herself from hoping it than she could stop herself from thinking and feeling at all.

❧ 16 ❧

After his conversation with Mrs. Cosgrove, Jacques had only stayed at Lady Heathcote's ball long enough to convince his father to leave.

The stern control he had been exercising over himself for years—what had kept him from attracting too much unwanted attention—was fraying quickly. The stress of discovering that the marquess had, somewhere in his memory, the power to undo Jacques and his father —to make social outcasts of them, if not something worse—was taking its toll, particularly as it had come at a time when Jacques was beginning to feel hopeful of a happy outcome with Miss Cosgrove.

Mrs. Cosgrove's words had been everything he knew but had been trying to pretend not to know: her daughter's reputation was of foremost importance, and Miss Cosgrove wouldn't be allowed to associate with anyone who could harm it in any way—much less marry such a person.

"What do we do?" Jacques said to his father as the carriage bobbled down the street.

His father was staring blankly at the seat across from him in the coach, but he looked up at Jacques's words.

"What *can* we do?" he said. The helpless, resigned note in his voice made Jacques clench his teeth.

Surely there must be *something* within their power? How could his father give up so easily?

Jacques cleared his throat, hoping to clear away the anger he felt toward his father. He knew it wasn't rational. His father had done what he had believed would give Jacques the best life possible. When Jacques thought on the alternatives, they were hardly better than the situation he currently faced.

Living in poverty in the war-torn streets of France? Or living in poverty in England, completely oblivious to the life he had experienced for the past twenty years, except perhaps as a servant?

But when he thought of losing Miss Cosgrove—of feeling so close to happiness, only to have it suddenly and mercilessly snatched from his reach—it made him wonder if never having known her or the world she operated in might not have been preferable.

He felt a wave of sympathy for Lady Caroline. Her rash and deranged behavior was no doubt brought on by a similar, helpless feeling of a widening distance from happiness with the man she loved. He could understand the desperation that, combined with a volatile temperament, might have led her to such a drastic action.

And yet, it had taken her no closer to the man she loved—further from him, likely.

And such was the case for Jacques. Nothing he did now could close the gap between him and the woman he loved.

"What will happen to us?" he said, turning his head to stare out the window at the passing houses.

"I wish I knew," said his father. "We will be cut, no doubt; no longer admitted among any of the people we now consider acquaintances." He let out a large breath. "Beyond that, I can hardly say. It will depend largely, no doubt, on how intent the Marquess of Retsford is upon revenging himself on you."

He was right. But who was to say whether the marquess would be content with their social ostracism? He certainly had enough power and influence to make life miserable for them in England—or worse, the power and influence to force them back to France.

They could hardly return to France. Jacques had heard enough about the plight of returned *émigrés* to know that they would hardly be better off there, particularly if it was known that they had impersonated noblemen for the last two decades.

There were no good options. And yet, how could they simply sit idly by, waiting for fate to deal them whatever blows it had in store?

Jacques rubbed his forehead harshly. His father had said that it was God who had given them the opportunity they took twenty years ago.

Where was God now?

❧ 17 ❧

As she and her parents stepped onto the grounds of the marquess's home which stood imposingly on the outskirts of London, Cecilia scanned the crowd of guests. Some were sitting on blankets, some standing under the white tents which had been raised for shade, and some walking among the boxwood hedges and roses beyond.

She knew that her eyes were searching in vain—of course the marquess would never have invited Lord Moulinet to the picnic—and yet she couldn't help herself. She hadn't seen or heard from him in days.

Her heart jumped as her gaze landed upon Letty and Aunt Emily. But there was no sign of the vicomte.

She stifled a sigh. This was hardly her idea of an enjoyable way to pass the day. It *would* have been, even two months ago. An invitation to one of the marquess's famous al fresco picnics? She would have been thrilled; victorious.

But the only thing that had brought her on this occasion was her mother's and father's insistence. How could she tell them that she had no intention of marrying the marquess, even if he offered for her?

"Ah, Cosgrove," said Lord Retsford as they reached the top of the stone staircase which led down to the picnic. "I am honored to have you here." He bowed slightly to Cecilia and her mother. Why did she always feel that there was a hint of mockery in his tone?

"Miss Cosgrove," he said, offering his arm, "allow me to show you the way to the food. I hope you will find it meets your expectations."

Taking his arm, she glanced at her parents and noted the pleased and triumphant glint in their eyes. It was the glint she had come to rely on, to crave, as it meant that they were proud of her. But today it only weighed her down.

The marquess led her down the steps, her parents trailing behind, surely surveying the crowd in the hopes that all eyes were turned to them to witness the honor which had been bestowed upon their daughter.

"It is my understanding," the marquess said, "from your cousin, that I have been so unfortunate as to incur your displeasure."

Cecilia felt a tightening in her chest, remembering Letty's escapade at Ranelagh Gardens. How was she to respond to such a blatant attack?

But he seemed to need no response from her. "She was very clear that you think my character reprehensible and"— he put a finger to his lips —"what was it that she said? Ah, yes, that I am far too old to be courting young ladies in their first blush of youth."

Cecilia tried to suppress a smile. She had never asked Letty precisely what she had said to the marquess. "And yet," she said, "you seem untroubled by her words."

"On the contrary," he said, "they inspired me with a greater desire to show forth my true character to you—to please where I have so far drawn your displeasure."

Cecilia looked over at him. He was watching her with a half-smile.

"Or perhaps," he said, "it is a lost cause. Perhaps you simply prefer the company of men like Lord Moulinet."

Cecilia bit back a rejoinder. Of course she preferred the vicomte's company to the marquess's.

"I wonder," said the marquess in a silky voice, "if perhaps you are not misled in your assumptions about both myself and the vicomte? It is entirely possible that *his* is the reprehensible character."

An inadvertent, scoffing laugh broke from Cecilia. "I think we are venturing into fantasy rather than reality, my lord."

"Hmm," he said, the same half-smile on his face. "We shall see, I suppose."

They arrived at the first white tent under which a long table of food and drink lay, spread with fruit and square-cut sandwiches, lemonade and ratafia, tarts and pies.

Cecilia glanced over her shoulder. Her parents had stopped just short of the tent and were watching her and the marquess, as though they hadn't wished to cut short the tête-à-tête they seemed to think Cecilia was enjoying. Her father winked at her, and Cecilia forced a smile.

Though she felt less and less dependent upon it, she was not immune to the desire to meet the expectations of her parents. Surely it wasn't wrong to wish to please one's parents. But what was one to do when it conflicted with one's own desires so significantly?

The marquess bowed and left her to the food, prompting her mother and father to step under the tent and approach.

"It is far better than we could ever have hoped, Cecilia," said her mother with a contented smile. She sighed slightly as she watched the marquess greeting other guests. "Lord Retsford! Of all people. And singling you out as he did."

"Yes," said her father, patting her shoulder, "you have done very well indeed, my dear."

Cecilia could only smile back. She had no one but herself to blame for the position she was in. The greatest irony of all was that her parents likely would have been content with a French Vicomte had she not persuaded them that she could aim as high as she pleased.

What had she done?

It was with unwonted joy that Cecilia greeted her sister Isabel upon her unexpected arrival in London the following day. Isabel and Charles had decided to break their journey in London after spending some time up north, and Cecilia felt an enormous sense of relief upon being informed of their presence.

Isabel had blinked in surprise at being greeted with such warmth and wrapped in such a hearty embrace by Cecilia. They had never been terribly close as sisters, but Cecilia's feelings toward Isabel had undergone a dramatic shift since last seeing her. She felt like a much-needed ally now.

Cecilia insisted upon helping Isabel get settled in, mentioning that she had a few dresses which she thought Isabel's darker complexion would do more justice to than had her own fair one. Isabel smiled confusedly and agreed to the plan, planting a kiss upon her husband's cheek and promising she would be down for dinner.

When Anaïs appeared at the door to Isabel's room, Cecilia thanked but dismissed her. "We will call for you when it is time to dress for dinner, but I should like to help Izzy with her belongings today."

Isabel had laughed softly upon overhearing this exchange. "What has come over you, Cecy?" she asked as she took out a dress from one of her valises.

"What do you mean?" said Cecilia, closing the door behind her. "I wish to spend time with my sister whom I haven't seen for almost two months. Surely that is nothing to surprise anyone?"

Isabel raised her brows, smoothing the skirts of the dress she had laid upon the bed. "Perhaps not—if you had ever sought out my company before today." She shot a teasing glance at Cecilia. "And offering to gift me dresses you dislike? It is all quite unprecedented, Cecy."

Cecilia slumped down onto the bed, surrendering to dramatics. "Izzy, you can have no notion how many things have happened since you left! And I am quite done up trying to decide how I am to go on."

Isabel's eyes flitted over to her. "Is this about Lady Caroline?"

"You know?"

Isabel shrugged. "I presume everyone does. We were at Charles's father's earlier today, and we had hardly been there an hour before the subject came up. It sounds quite shocking."

Cecilia clasped her hands, rubbing her fingers along her skin. "It *was*. And Mama insists that I have nothing more to do with her."

"And what do *you* think?"

Cecilia sighed. "I am not sure what to think. Which is why I have needed you so much. Lady Caroline is my friend, but there is no denying that her behavior is, more often than not, very shocking and indiscreet."

Isabel didn't meet her eyes as she placed a pair of gloves in the armoire. "Do you worry that you will be tainted by association with her?"

Cecilia frowned. "It sounds quite terrible when you phrase it in such a way, but I suppose the answer is yes."

Isabel turned to look at her and then came to sit down beside her. "Why is Lady Caroline your friend?"

Cecilia stared at her sister. "What ever do you mean?"

"Simply that," she said blankly. "Why did you befriend Lady Caroline—or accept the friendship she extended to you?"

Cecilia squinted, as if it might help her understand what her own thoughts and intentions had been when it had all started. "Lady Caroline appeared quite unexpectedly in my life at a time when I needed her influence." Seeing Isabel begin to speak, Cecilia waved her hand to stop her. "I don't mean her social influence. I mean her confidence, her unconcern for society's opinions. I had never met anyone so very free, you know? And with such a desirable life— married to the future Lord Melbourne, brought up in Devonshire

House, madly in love with Lord Byron, doing just as she pleases." She let out a large breath.

Isabel smiled sadly at her. "I can see how she must have appeared very enviable to you. But I think it is quite apparent that she is not at all happy in her life. In fact, it all seems very tragic."

Cecilia nodded. Lady Caroline's marriage had been an advantageous one, but it had clearly not brought her happiness.

For so long, Cecilia had acted under the assumption that, if she were able to acquire enough influence, she would somehow reach a pinnacle of contentment where she would remain for the rest of her life, subsisting on the admiration of others. But such admiration and influence had come to seem fickle and fleeting, holding much less interest for Cecilia than the prospect of a life beside someone she loved.

"Mama and Papa are very set upon my marrying Lord Retsford," she said, staring down at her hands.

Isabel's head jerked back. "The marquess? He is quite old isn't he? And a bit of a rake, I thought."

Cecilia only grimaced.

Isabel took her hand in hers. "But you have always wished to marry a peer, Cecy. And you can hardly do better than a marquess." She squeezed Cecilia's hand and winked at her.

Cecilia smiled wryly. "Perhaps a duke?" She laughed softly. "I *did* always wish to make as brilliant a match as I could. But I suppose that I never anticipated that I would fall in love." She stole a glance at Isabel, whose eyes widened considerably.

"In love?" She scooted closer to Cecilia. "You must tell me everything, then, of course. From the very beginning."

"Didn't you tell Charles you would be down shortly?"

Isabel waved a dismissive hand. "He and Tobias are surely entertaining themselves well enough."

Cecilia felt a tingling warmth fill her chest. How had she been ignorant for so many years of her sister's sweet nature? It had taken Isabel's marriage for Cecilia to appreciate her.

She recounted, from the beginning, meeting Lord Moulinet—his apparent disdain for her, his blatant criticism of the affectation he perceived in her manner, and the slow shift that had taken Cecilia from pique to respect to love. When Cecilia recounted what had occurred at the prize fight, Isabel's hand flew to her mouth.

"Good heavens, Cecy! He put himself at great risk for you and Lady Caroline—but how very awkward it all is." She stood and paced the room. "It is very unfortunate, for absent Lord Retsford, I think Mama and Papa would be very happy indeed to give their blessing to your marriage with a French nobleman."

Cecilia nodded. "It is even more unfortunate than you know, Izzy, for I think that Lord Retsford has tired of me—undoubtedly due to some failing of mine, Mama will say—and that he only pays me any attention as a way of revenging himself upon Lord Moulinet."

Isabel made an expression of disgust. "How terribly vindictive of him. And risky! What should he do if you had fallen in love with him and had come to expect his offer?"

"I suppose he knows well enough that I have no real interest in marrying him."

Isabel's mouth twisted to the side, and she put a fist to her mouth. "But as long as he continues to show any indication of interest in courting you—however shameful his reasoning for doing so—Mama and Papa will hold out hope for a match." She straightened. "If we can rid them of that hope, though, I think they would look kindly upon Lord Moulinet's suit, would they not?"

Cecilia tilted her head from side to side. "There is an English Viscount who has paid me no little attention—and I think they might prefer him to a French Vicomte, particularly since the Revolution has so drastically changed the fortunes of French nobles."

"Good gracious, Cecy," said Isabel with a laugh, "you may as well have the entire English peerage courting you." She came to sit down again beside her. "I am afraid that it may come down to a choice for you—and an undesirable one."

Cecilia swallowed but inclined her head to invite Isabel to continue.

"You may have to choose between pursuing your own desires and satisfying Mama and Papa." She clenched her teeth. "Papa may writhe and yell and threaten to withhold your dowry, but it is you who, at the end of the day, has to live your life by the side of your husband. If he is someone you love and respect, I believe you might weather any storm together and still be happy. If he is someone you despise even now"— her shoulders came up and then slumped down —"you may end up as torn and desperate as Lady Caroline."

She clasped Cecilia's hands between her own for a moment and then stood, walking to the door.

She paused at the threshold and looked over her shoulder at Cecilia. "One more thing, Cecy. You said that Lady Caroline came into your life when you needed her most. Perhaps it is your turn to return the favor."

❦ 18 ❧

Jacques had considered fleeing. The thought of making it harder for the marquess to carry out his plans—for Jacques harbored little doubt that he would remember where he knew them from—of avoiding the repercussions that would be most harsh in town...it was appealing. Or would the marquess simply use what he knew as a means of intimidation? As a way of ensuring that his path to Miss Cosgrove was free of Jacques?

But in the end, Jacques couldn't bring himself to cower and hide. Not from the marquess. It would give the man too much satisfaction —to make him feel as though he had won.

They only had a week left in town, in any case. And for Jacques and his father to absent themselves from the dinner party the Broussards were hosting would be to give great offense to a family Jacques cared for deeply.

No, they would carry on as usual and fight for their dignity.

So it was that, as he dressed for the dinner party, Jacques's hands only trembled slightly as he tied his cravat. He was resigned to his fate and determined to spend whatever time he had left showing his gratitude to the people he had come to love. His greatest hope was that, after the shock wore off, they would remember him with fondness rather than disgust.

His resolution wavered only once, when he saw Miss Cosgrove walk in, preceded by her parents, flanked by her brother, and followed by her sister and her sister's husband.

Miss Cosgrove looked magnificent in her pale blue crepe evening gown, with a simple white riband woven through her hair. Without even being near, he could imagine the jasmine scent which clung about her wherever she went.

What would she think of him? He wanted to keep her from the truth for as long as he could, and yet he was anxious to see her reaction. Would she be disgusted to learn of his humble origins? Grateful to have avoided marriage to him? Or would her eyes water with betrayal and hurt?

Jacques was hardly surprised when the Marquess of Retsford arrived, but he swallowed as he saw the victorious tilt of the man's chin, his air of calm self-assurance, and the knowing glance he cast at Jacques.

Jacques straightened himself and held the marquess's eyes. What would have happened if he had never stirred the marquess's anger? If he had not involved himself at the prize fight?

But Jacques could hardly regret saving Miss Cosgrove's reputation.

The marquess approached him with a slight nod. "Good evening, *Lord* Moulinet."

"Good evening," Jacques replied, ignoring the mocking tone.

"I hope that you will enjoy this evening," Lord Retsford said, a slight sneer tainting the smile on his mouth. He leaned in toward Jacques and whispered. "Rest assured, it will be your last such opportunity."

Jacques's muscles tensed, but the marquess walked away, giving him no opportunity to respond, even if he had found something to say.

So this was it? The marquess intended to reveal what he knew tonight? Jacques had wondered if Lord Retsford wouldn't have preferred the wider audience afforded by a ball or some other public gathering. But apparently not.

Jacques looked around at the company in the room—at everyone whose opinion he cared for, all the people he had come to love as his own family.

The marquess could hardly have chosen a more poignant audience.

He knew a new impulse to run, to escape. But he had to face the Broussards—surely he owed it to look them in the eye after the years of life they had shared together. And he had to face Miss Cosgrove.

He walked to his father and whispered, "The marquess has come with one aim alone. You had best prepare yourself, Father."

His father nodded, the same determined expression on his face that Jacques imagined was on his own. "Then I shall need a drink," his father said, walking in the direction of a bottle of brandy.

"Lord Moulinet." The voice came from behind him, slightly tentative, painfully familiar. He closed his eyes for a brief moment and took in a fortifying breath—laced with jasmine—before turning toward Miss Cosgrove.

Her smile for him was different this evening. It was shy and almost conspiratorial, as if they shared a secret of mutual affection but she was unsure if she had understood properly. And her eyes? They looked at him with the warmth he had seen growing for weeks.

It was enough to make him reckless—to give rise to a desire to take her by the hand, tell her everything, and ask her to run away with him, somewhere where the marquess couldn't hurt them.

But Jacques blinked, and the vision was gone. It was impossible.

"I wished to introduce you," said Miss Cosgrove, "to my sister and her husband, Mrs. Isabel Galbraith and Mr. Charles Galbraith. They are in town breaking their journey for a few days."

He bowed politely, very aware of the direct, measuring gaze of Mrs. Galbraith.

There was a drawn out pause after the introduction, until Letty bounced over to them, putting a hand on Jacques's arm. Mr. and Mrs. Galbraith were approached by Aunt Emily and turned away.

"Jacques," she said, "I had no idea that you and the marquess were acquainted before! You never said a word."

Jacques stiffened slightly.

"Perhaps you had forgotten," Letty suggested, "for he said that you were only a boy, just arrived from France. And I can't say that I blame you if that is the case"— she leaned in toward him with her mischievous smile —"for who would *wish* to remember him?"

Jacques's eyes darted to the marquess who was watching Letty with satisfaction. He was taking no small pleasure in taunting Jacques.

"I had not remembered, to be quite honest," said Jacques truthfully, "but it was a tumultuous time."

Miss Cosgrove was looking at him with raised brows. "Does his dislike of you stretch back that far?"

He looked down at her, scanning her face, hoping to take in every detail—her deep blue eyes, her soft pink lips and matching cheeks, the way one stray curl had dropped onto her forehead—before the intimacy of her demeanor disappeared. "I imagine his dislike of me stems from the moment he began to see me as a competitor for your affection."

She laughed softly and swallowed, meeting his eyes with an intensity that made the hairs on Jacques's neck stand on end. "The marquess never stood a chance against you," she said.

Jacques's heart felt at once somehow heavy and light, and with everything inside him, he wished to take the woman in front of him in his arms and show her how he felt.

"I should think not," Letty said. "For not even a marquessate can make up for all his disagreeableness and insufferable behavior."

The dinner bell rang out, and the company began moving toward the door.

Miss Cosgrove looked up at Jacques, the side of her mouth turning up. "Well, my lord," she said in a timid voice, "are you going to accompany me in to dinner, or shall you leave me to go in alone—or worse, on the arm of Lord Retsford?"

Jacques chuckled. "I would be honored, Miss Cosgrove." He performed an exaggerated bow, eliciting a delighted smile from her, and then extended his arm. The niggling discomfort and guilt he forcefully suppressed. He could not resist Miss Cosgrove this evening, no matter what she asked of him.

The marquess looked on from the other side of the room, his nostrils flared but his mouth drawn out in a mocking smile.

Lord Retsford sat next to Mrs. Broussard near the head of the table, while Jacques helped Miss Cosgrove into the seat beside him. The looks they exchanged with each interaction would surely haunt Jacques forever—emblazoned on his memory as a reminder of what almost was but could never be.

Somehow that knowledge made her lashed looks, her intimate smiles, and the brushes of their arms against one another all the more sweet—achingly so.

If only he could have explained himself to her—or let her know how he felt. He never wished her to doubt that his feelings for her were real, even if nothing else was.

"Perhaps this is not the place for it," said Miss Cosgrove in a low voice, "but we were never given the chance to finish our conversation at Lady Heathcote's ball. You wished to tell me something important, did you not?"

His heart sank. "Yes," he said, glancing at Lord Retsford, "but I think that it is perhaps too late."

Her forehead wrinkled. "Too late?"

He clenched his fists, the feeling of powerlessness descending upon him and smothering him. He clenched his eyes shut. "I wish I could explain everything to you, but you *must* know that what I feel for you is real. Promise me that you will not forget that."

She blinked rapidly, her eyes alert as she nodded. "You alarm me," she said with a swallow.

Aunt Emily stood at the head of the table, signaling the women to follow her to the drawing room.

Miss Cosgrove leaned in toward Jacques and said in a whisper. "Meet me in ten minutes in the alcove down the corridor."

Jacques stiffened, hesitating. A clandestine meeting would hardly be wise, particularly when he felt the eyes of the marquess on him.

"Please," Miss Cosgrove said urgently as she stood.

Realizing that Miss Cosgrove was the only one remaining at the table and would likely attract attention if she remained any longer, Jacques nodded once, grimacing, and she left with a small smile of relief.

He shut his eyes. How in the world would he manage to leave the room without attracting undue attention? And what if they were discovered? Once Miss Cosgrove discovered the truth about him, the memory of such a meeting would only add insult to injury.

He debated within himself, torn between two unpalatable options. He could hardly leave her to await his arrival in the corridor when he had agreed to meet her there. But the thought of going felt wrong, too.

He heaved a sigh. He would simply have to meet her to say that he didn't wish to compromise her at all by engaging in secretive conduct—particularly in his aunt's home.

The hands of the tall clock seemed to tick at half-speed for the next few minutes as he sat at the table, forcing himself to drink the port in front of him despite the complete lack of appetite for it.

When ten minutes had passed, he leaned over to his father and excused himself.

As Jacques rose, he noted how the marquess's eyes watched him leave the room.

Jacques's mouth drew into a grim line as he walked down the corridor. It was tempting to use the opportunity to explain things to Miss Cosgrove—to prepare her for what she would no doubt hear, whether from the marquess or from someone else.

He caught sight of Miss Cosgrove, standing in the alcove next to the tall damask curtains, her hands clasped in front of her.

"Miss Cosgrove," he said, coming before her, "I cannot think this wise—"

She dropped her hands and closed the final gap between them, reaching her hands up to his face and pulling his lips down to hers.

Stunned, Jacques froze for a moment, knowing he should pull back, should stop such an imprudent action, but feeling the warmth of her hands on his cheeks, the softness of her lips pressed to his.

And before he had even consciously decided anything, his arms were wrapped around her, pulling her closer, his mouth moving with hers in concert, urgent and imperative, as if he could say everything he needed to say without any words at all.

He finally pulled back, his chest rising and falling rapidly, as he closed his eyes in an effort to right the world around him which seemed to be spinning. "We cannot...I cannot..."

He dropped his arms from around her waist and opened his eyes, hardly daring to look at Miss Cosgrove, at the woman he loved but couldn't have.

"You can have no notion," she said softly, brushing at his forehead softly with her fingers, a smile trembling on her lips, "how long I have been wishing to do that."

He stifled a groan. He wished he had done it before—wished he had kissed her a hundred times—and yet he knew that this one kiss would torment him forever.

"This is a mistake, Miss Cosgrove," he said, shaking his head and taking a step back. "I would not risk your reputation this way." He looked at her searching blue eyes and the way they looked up at him with such care and desire.

"Call me Cecilia," she said. "And, to be fair, *I* was the one who risked my reputation. Not you."

He clenched his fists, willing himself to look away from her lips, to forget the way his hand had fit perfectly in the small of her back and how her hand had cradled his cheek. "Much as I might wish to stay with you here in this alcove all night, I cannot. You don't understand."

She looked at him, confusion overtaking the warmth in her eyes. "No, I don't," she said. "What is the matter? What troubles you so?"

His mouth drew into a tight line. What could he possibly say? There was no time. "I am not who you think I am," he said.

A door opened down the corridor, and his head whipped around. The other men were no doubt making their way to the drawing room.

"I can't explain it all right now," he said, his neck tightening in frustration. Why had he not garnered the courage to tell her before? "Please," he said in a supplicating voice, "remember what I told you. Know that I would do anything to make you happy and"— he exhaled —"that I am more sorry than you will ever know."

The sound of muffled voices growing louder met Jacques's ears and he nodded down the corridor toward the drawing room. "You must go," he said, swallowing at the pitiful bewilderment in Cecilia's eyes as they held his. "Go!" he said, and she whipped around, rushing down the hallway and into the drawing room.

Jacques walked down the corridor, rubbing his forehead. He almost wished he could persuade the marquess to do his worst and to do it right away. The suspense and tension as he awaited the revelation hung over his head like a leaden weight.

He stepped into the group of men, coming shoulder-to-shoulder with his father. Neither of them said a word as they entered the drawing room.

Cecilia stood next to her sister and brother-in-law, but her attention was clearly not on the conversation—her eyes were glazed over and staring blankly ahead of her.

The hands of the clock continued moving, with no sign from the marquess of any intention of interrupting the conversations being held among the people in the room. When a request was made that Letty favor the company with a song on the pianoforte, she walked over to the piano, only to pause as the door to the drawing room opened to reveal one of the Broussard footmen. He walked over to

Mr. Broussard, leaning in to confer with him privately, all the while with Letty sitting at the pianoforte, hands paused on the keys.

Mr. Broussard frowned and nodded, and the footman left. "Lord Retsford," said Mr. Broussard, standing and walking over to him. He leaned in, putting a hand over his mouth to shield whatever he was communicating, and then looked at the marquess, shrugging as though he didn't know what to make of the message he bore.

Jacques watched with an ever-increasing heart rate as Lord Retsford's eyes moved to him, triumphant and glinting. Mr. Broussard returned to his seat, and nodded to Letty who prepared herself to begin, only to be interrupted again by the marquess.

"I hesitate," said the marquess, "to postpone the delight in store for us thanks to Miss Broussard's accomplishment at the pianoforte, but I cannot in good conscience hold my tongue any longer—not when we are all in the company of impostors."

The air in the room stilled, eyes shifting from side to side in confusion, and Jacques held himself straight, ignoring the impulse he had to watch for Cecilia's reaction. The marquess nodded to confirm his words.

"Among us here are two people who have duped us all for years— decades even—masquerading as our equals, taking advantage of our kindness when they are, in fact, no better than scoundrels and criminals. This very moment, one of them ingratiates himself with a member of our company, while she, oblivious to the truth, accepts these advances, even returns them, unsuspecting that the man she sits beside is nothing but an actor and a snake—a murderer, even."

Sharp intakes of breath sounded all around Jacques, and he clenched his jaw. He had been concerned about being revealed for the impostor he was, but he had never considered that the marquess might accuse him and his father of having murdered the Comte de Montreuil.

"This man"—he said, pointing to Jacques's father —"is not the Comte de Montreuil. And this man"—he pointed to Jacques —"is not the Vicomte de Moulinet. I met them more than twenty years ago when they landed at Dover as servant *émigrés* in the service of the *true* Comte. Blackguards that they are, they saw their opportunity and murdered the poor Comte"— more exclamations of shock sounded around the table —"and then used me as their first dupe, pretending to request my assistance in reviving the Comte, when they wished him dead so that they could take his money, his good name, and his title, deceiving us all to this very day."

Jacques could feel Cecilia's eyes on him, but he had to force himself to meet them.

She looked at him, incredulity and shock warring in her eyes. "My lord?" she said.

The marquess scoffed. "Hardly. He is nothing but a commoner."

Cecilia laughed nervously at the marquess's words. "Impossible." She looked to Jacques. "Tell him it's impossible, Lord Moulinet. Tell everyone that he is simply jealous of you and has been for weeks."

Jacques said nothing, swallowing as though it would rid him of the emotion threatening to overcome him at the sight of Cecilia defending him.

"What he says is true," he finally managed, unable to watch her reaction. He moved his eyes to Aunt Emily—the woman who had taken them in and made sure they learned English and had a home until they were able to purchase their own. He saw the same confused horror in her eyes that penetrated him from all sides. "But we are *not* murderers. That is entirely false."

"And you expect us to believe you?" said the marquess with a mocking laugh.

Jacques looked to his father, who stood emotionless and still next to him. He looked to Cecilia, and his heart lurched at the betrayal written in her eyes.

She shook her head, backing up one step. "And you had the audacity to lecture *me* about masks?"

Jacques lifted his palms and then dropped them. She was right.

"Both of you"— the marquess looked down at the paper he was holding —"apparently Jacques and Hugo Levesque by name—are in violation of the Aliens Act and will be deported after standing before the magistrate."

Jacques's head swam, his eyes unfocused and the pricks of candlelight throughout the room swaying oddly. He felt his father's arm tremble next to him.

The marquess lowered the paper, looking at Jacques with a hard stare. "Two constables stand outside this door, waiting to escort you to Newgate. If you are so unwise as to attempt an escape, they have brought instruments to ensure your cooperation."

Jacques stared ahead, resisting the impulse to apologize to his aunt and uncle. To Letty. To Cecilia. It would only ring false in their ears.

With a swooshing sound, Cecilia fled from the room.

He shut his eyes. He would never see her again.

Footsteps sounded, and Jacques opened his eyes to see the marquess welcome the constables: two bulky men with large cudgels hanging from leather belts at their waists. They grabbed Jacques and his father by the arm, pulling them from the spot they had stood rooted to for several minutes.

Jacques scanned the faces of the Broussards one final time: his uncle frowning deeply, Aunt Emily's head turned away, and Letty's wide, fearful eyes blinking slowly as she sat before the pianoforte.

He would miss Letty terribly.

❧ 19 ❧

Cecilia had not returned to the drawing room after Lord
Retsford's revelation. She hadn't been able to bear the
thought of meeting anyone's eyes without bursting into
tears—tears of anger, tears of hurt, tears of disgust; she hardly knew
what she was feeling.

It all still felt like a dream. A terrible, impossible dream. She had
fallen in love with an imposter? A criminal? A *murderer*?

It was too fantastic to believe. If Lord Moulinet—or Mr.
Levesque, rather—was a murderer, surely anyone could be one?
There was nothing of the murderer about his calm, gentle demeanor.
There was no trace of the commoner in him, refined and easy as his
manners were.

And yet, he had admitted the truth of the marquess's revelation—
or at least most of it. But what was she to believe from someone
whose entire life was a lie and a sham?

She had sat wordless, staring out of the coach window on the
carriage ride back to Belport Street, clenching her eyes shut as her
mother talked without stopping of the scandal they had just
witnessed.

"I cannot say I am surprised," she had said, "for I always felt there was something not right about him. And his father? What kind of true Comte would dress in such a vulgarly colorful manner?"

Isabel's hand had found Cecilia's, and she had squeezed it gently.

Cecilia tossed and turned all night, unable to suppress the memory of the moments she and Mr. Levesque had shared in the alcove, his words sounding over and over again in her ears: *"You must know that what I feel for you is real."*

How could she believe such a thing? And even if it were true, what then? He was nothing but the servant of a dead French comte.

When she awoke in the morning, her head throbbed, and she put a gentle finger to the swollen bags under her eyes.

She pulled up the linens over her head, wishing she could sleep forever, wishing she could avoid the necessity of facing her emotions and untangling them.

She needed to occupy herself with anything other than her own problems.

She sat up in bed, Isabel's words coming to her: *"Perhaps it is your turn to return the favor."* She hadn't spoken with Lady Caroline since the episode at Lady Heathcote's. How was she faring?

Pulling back her bedcovers, Cecilia slid out of bed and walked to the small écritoire next to the window. She sat down and dipped the quill in the ink, letting the feather brush her cheek until finally putting the quill to paper and scrawling away.

Cecilia's mother would heavily disapprove of her plan, worried for the damage it might do to her reputation and prospects. But Cecilia was tired of worrying over such things.

It would do Lady Caroline good to take air with Cecilia, and it would surely do Cecilia good. Of course they would attract attention —the town was still gossiping about what Lady Caroline had done. No doubt the discovery of last night's revelation would quickly put the episode out of everyone's thoughts in favor of the new scandal the town was always craving.

Whiling away the time until she would receive a response from

Lady Caroline, Cecilia sat in the morning room, fidgeting with the tassels of the gold pillow she held and staring blankly at the window across the room, when Letty walked in unannounced.

Cecilia looked up in surprise, and Letty rushed over to her, untying the ribbons of her bonnet and pulling it from her head. "Cecy," she said in her most dramatic voice. She sat down beside her and enfolded her in an embrace.

Cecilia returned it but soon drew back, her nose wrinkling. "Letty, you smell of spirits!"

Letty laughed, setting her bonnet down beside her.

"Letty," said Cecilia suspiciously, "*why* do you smell of spirits?"

"Nevermind that, Cecy," Letty said impatiently. "I have come to talk to you about Jacques."

Cecilia turned her head away. "What is there to discuss?"

"What is there to disc—" she blinked at Cecilia, uncomprehending. "We *cannot* allow them to ship him and my uncle back to France, Cecy!"

"He is *not* your uncle, Letty," Cecilia said, her voice more biting than she had intended.

"Perhaps not by blood," said Letty, thrusting her chin out, "but certainly he has treated me more like an uncle than *your* father."

Cecilia said nothing, only letting out a frustrated breath. Letty was right. The connection she had to the Levesques was undeniable.

Letty looked at Cecilia, her eyes narrowing, and her forehead wrinkling. "You don't even *care* what becomes of them, do you?" She shook her head in disgust. "And here I've been thinking you were in love with Jacques." She stood, snatching the bonnet from beside her and staring at Cecilia as she took two steps back and turned toward the door.

"Letty, wait," Cecilia said.

Letty turned toward her, her shoulders down and her chest thrust out in defiance. "What?"

Cecilia's shoulder came up helplessly. "What can we possibly do? They are *murderers*."

An impatient huff blew through Letty's nostrils. "Of course they aren't."

"How can you know that?"

"Because I know them." Letty's neck stretched to its full height. "And because I asked them."

Cecilia frowned. "How? Mama says they were taken straight to Newgate last night."

She shrugged. "I went to ask them myself."

Eyes widening, Cecilia said in disbelief, "You went to Newgate?"

Letty nodded again. "Unfortunately, one of the other prisoners spilled his drink on me as I was leaving. I admit, it is not the kind of place I should like to visit regularly."

"I should think not," Cecilia cried. Her eyes flitted down to Letty's dress. "So *that* is why you smell of spirits? Good heavens, Letty! What could you have been thinking? It is terribly dangerous, not to mention entirely reckless! Have you no care for your reputation? Or your life?"

"Well no one *did* see me," she said, crossing her arms, "and I hardly regard the danger when my own dear Jacques is set to be tried in two days! Besides," she sniffed, "if you must know, Mama came with me. You know she has always been terribly fond of Jacques, and she was intent on giving him and my uncle the chance to explain themselves. *She* believes them!"

"And your father?" Cecilia said.

Letty waved him away with a dismissive hand. "He would, too, if he would only lend an ear to them for even a moment! But he won't, and there is no time to convince him." She shut her eyes, and tears squeezed from them. "Oh, Cecy, we *must* not let it happen!"

"Letty," Cecilia said softly, pitifully, "there is nothing we can do."

"I think if you truly loved him," Letty sniffled, "you would do everything you could to stop him from being sent away. He is still Jacques, Cecy! Even if he was born poor." She shook her head at Cecilia. "I thought I could surely count on *you* to do something. Or at the very least to be present for his trial."

Cecilia was the recipient of one last glance full of betrayal before Letty rushed from the room, slamming the door behind her.

Cecilia sank back onto the cushions, rubbing her forehead.

Letty had gone to Newgate to see the Levesques? She couldn't help but admire Letty's loyalty to her cousin and uncle.

But how could Letty look on the treachery with so little hurt or anger?

If Cecilia was being honest with herself, Letty's accusations against her had stung.

The door opened again, and Cecilia closed her eyes and sighed, expecting more of Letty's dramatics.

But it was the footman, holding a letter on a tray. Cecilia immediately recognized the script of Lady Caroline and opened the note greedily, her eyes taking in the few lines within seconds. She stepped into the drawing room to look at the hands of the clock which showed one in the afternoon.

She hurried up the stairs, anxious to change into her walking dress so that Lady Caroline wouldn't be left waiting when she arrived in half an hour.

A short time later, Cecilia stepped quietly through the front door, satisfied that she had not attracted the attention of her mother. She smiled at Lady Caroline, sitting composedly in the seat of her high-perch phaeton. She looked skinnier than ever, but she was beaming down at Cecilia.

When Cecilia stepped up into the phaeton and settled in, smoothing her skirt and fixing the tilt of her bonnet, Lady Caroline cocked her head slightly.

"Oh dear," Lady Caroline said, taking Cecilia's hand. "What has happened?"

Cecilia sighed. "Do I look so terrible that it is that obvious?"

Lady Caroline gave her hand a squeeze. "You could never look terrible. Only sad, or tired perhaps?" She inspected Cecilia's face through slightly narrowed eyes. "Nevermind, we shall discuss it all as we drive." She arranged the reins in her hands and then gave them a flick, sending the phaeton forward.

Lady Caroline took them through the busy streets of the town, saying, "Do not think that I am ignorant of what it means for you to sit up beside me here after what happened at Lady Heathcote's." She took her eyes off the road for a brief, appreciative glance at Cecilia. "You are very kind, Cecilia."

Cecilia shook her head, uncomfortably aware that it was Isabel rather than herself who had perceived the opportunity to be a true friend. "I am not nearly as kind as you think I am. In fact, I am terribly selfish."

"If that were true, you would not be sitting beside a woman believed to be mad and obsessed and dangerous."

They entered the less crowded lane of the park, where Lady Caroline finally relaxed her shoulders and said, "Now, tell me all."

Cecilia's recounting of the events of the night before sounded jumbled and tangential even to her own ears, but she hardly knew how to convey everything that had happened without clarifying and providing context to Lady Caroline. When she came to the part of the story that included her exchange with Mr. Levesque in the alcove, she tried to gloss over the specifics, but Lady Caroline smiled mischievously at her, unfooled by the vague nature of Cecilia's description.

When she reached the marquess's revelation, Lady Caroline exclaimed. "How very famous!"

Taken aback and somewhat offended at the uncomprehending nature of Lady Caroline's reaction, Cecilia doubled back and looked at her friend. Lady Caroline met her eyes and laughed.

"It is precisely the type of adventure I myself should wish to have if I had been born into their circumstances."

Baffled at the lighthearted way in which Lady Caroline seemed to regard the discovery which had sent Cecilia reeling, she found herself without words.

"But please," Lady Caroline said, "continue. It was very rude of me to interrupt."

Cecilia's mouth opened and closed. "But that is it. I left before the constables could escort him and his father to Newgate from where they will be sent back to France."

"Oh dear," said Lady Caroline, finally beginning to show proper signs of comprehending what had occurred to overset Cecilia so entirely. She reined in the horses, pulling the phaeton to the side of the lane and turning toward Cecilia. "And what of you?"

"What *of* me?" Cecilia said.

Lady Caroline raised her brows. "Does knowing of the vicomte's circumstances alter your love for him?"

Cecilia swallowed and frowned at the direct question. She hardly knew how to answer. "He is not a Vicomte," she said in a sullen voice.

Lady Caroline shrugged. "And if he is not? Surely it was not his title you fell in love with, or else you should have more easily fallen in love with the marquess." She shot Cecilia a significant look to drive home her point. "So the question remains: do you still love him?"

"Of course not!" Cecilia cried.

Lady Caroline raised a single brow.

"I don't know!" Cecilia said evasively. "But what does it matter? Surely you see that I could not marry a man who betrayed me so, much less one who is a poor Frenchman."

Lady Caroline tilted her head to the side. "Why not?" She put a hand up to silence Cecilia. "You may pretend that you have no choice in the matter, my dear, but we always have a choice."

Cecilia scoffed. "And you think I should immediately forgive a murderer?"

Lady Caroline looked at her skeptically. "Surely you don't truly believe that? The vicomte himself refuted that allegation."

"And we are to trust him at his word when he has been lying for decades?"

"*I* certainly do," said Lady Caroline, "for why should he admit to everything *but* the murder charge?"

Cecilia wrung her hands. Of course if she had to choose between believing the marquess and believing Mr. Levesque, she would still believe the latter. But... "Murderer or not, he is still the man who made me fall in love with him under false pretenses."

"Cecilia, Cecilia," said Lady Caroline, "we all deceive each other to one extent or another. How can you be so sure that you would have acted any differently in his shoes? We all jump at the opportunity to increase our power, influence, and comfort, and with much less a case for doing so. Recall that he has been over twenty years living the life of a Vicomte, to say nothing of him being roped into the deception when he was only a child! I imagine it hardly seemed a part by the time he met you. Besides, it is not as if he set out to betray you purposefully. Indeed, it sounds as though he wished to tell you of his circumstances on more than one occasion."

Cecilia sniffed, unsure what to make of Lady Caroline's words and very nearly certain that she was right.

"In any case," Lady Caroline continued, "he may have fooled us all into believing him a Vicomte, but I can tell you with certainty that his ability to play a part was not such that he could fool me into believing he loved you when he did not."

Cecilia's heart jumped inside her, the traitorous organ.

"And of course," Lady Caroline said, sending Cecilia a sidelong glance with a hint of censure, "you must realize that the only reason he was discovered was because of *you*." She tilted her head from side to side. "And me. The marquess would likely never have made an effort to take revenge upon the vicomte if it were not for the vicomte stepping in to save us both at the prize fight. We owe him a great deal. Pauper or noble, he has saved my life on no less than three occasions."

Cecilia's conscience pricked her, and she felt a moment's irritation. She had hoped to receive consolation from Lady Caroline, to be met with shared anger at the vicomte's deception; but so far from condemning the vicomte, Lady Caroline was defending him in every way possible, and making Cecilia feel as though *she* were the traitorous one.

"Do you love him still, Cecilia?" Lady Caroline asked, her tone softer and more understanding. "That is what you must decide. And if you do love him, do you wish to *do* something about it?"

Cecilia wrung her hands, her eyes stinging as she reflected on the joy she had felt over the past two months. It was always connected with *him*.

Lady Caroline sighed. "Allow me to put a question to you which I think may help make sense of what your true feelings are."

Cecilia nodded and swallowed.

"If the Victomte—yes, I insist on calling him that, for he is more like a Vicomte than any of the *real* Vicomtes I know—if he had told you the truth, but you knew without a doubt that you could live out the rest of your lives together with no one the wiser about his low birth, would you have married him?"

Cecilia shifted in her chair, wiping a tear from her cheek. What was the answer to that piercing question? If she said yes, it would be an admission that she cared only for society's *opinion* of Mr. Levesque's humble beginnings rather than the beginnings them-selves. If she said no, then what kind of love did she have for him?

"Yes, I would have," she sobbed.

Lady Caroline patted her hand. "I am glad to hear that."

Cecilia held her palms up on her lap. "But what does it matter, Caro? He is to be shipped off to France, and I shall never see him again."

Lady Caroline looked at Cecilia calculatingly. "I must ask you one more question, then. If he were *not* shipped off to France, would you be willing to ally yourself with him, despite his loss of status, despite the fact that he will be ostracized and cut from society? Would you risk yourself to be with him?"

Cecilia's face crumpled, and she nodded, unable to speak.

Lady Caroline nodded officially. "*That* is what I needed to know: that your love is the type that is willing to endure humiliation for the sake of its object."

"But how does that help us?"

Lady Caroline smiled enigmatically. "It does. That is all I may say for the moment."

And with such an indecipherable remark, Lady Caroline turned the conversation to other avenues, leaving Cecilia feeling even less comforted than at the beginning of their ride, as she had now admitted to her true emotions but felt more powerless than ever to act upon them.

❧ 20 ❧

Jacques shifted his legs which were stretched out on the floor, the sound of clanking irons echoing in the prison cell as he did so. He raked a hand through his disheveled hair and glanced at his father, who lay upon the sole bed in the cell. He had been sleeping quite a bit since their arrival, likely so lost to hope as to feel sapped of energy.

It was true that there was little hope at all. With the marquess against them, there was hardly anything Jacques could say to defend against his influence and power.

His timing had been well-planned indeed, with Middlesex Quarter Sessions set to take place just two days after their arrival at Newgate. And while Jacques was relieved at the knowledge that their time in Newgate would be short, he hardly looked forward with pleasure at the prospect of being deported to France. There was no doubt in his mind that such would be the result of their trial. The marquess would ensure it.

Jacques let out a wry chuckle as he thought of Letty and Aunt Emily's visit two days since. He had initially been too shocked upon seeing them, too relieved that they didn't despise him, to cry out at their coming to the prison. And even when he insisted that Letty return home without delay, she had scoffed, teasing that he could hardly force her when he was behind bars.

Jacques had been touched at her insistence that she would do everything she could to ensure they were *not* deported, but her naïve hope had not resulted in the optimism she had clearly expected to see from him.

Aunt Emily had been much more reserved on arrival at their cell. It was clear to Jacques that she was unsure *what* to believe. But, as Jacques had recounted their story, she had softened to the point of tears.

The visit had been a needed salve on Jacques's hurting conscience and his wounded soul. Aunt Emily and Letty, at least, still cared for them, despite knowing their origins. Nor did they believe them to be the murderers the marquess had accused them of being.

His father stirred and then sat up, no doubt wakened by the grating of his irons against one another.

"They should be here soon, I imagine," said Jacques, staring blankly ahead. "It must be nigh on two, and that is when the trial is set for."

His father only nodded and sat at the edge of the hard bed.

Jacques could hardly bear to look at his father. Gone was the vivacious, colorful personality of the last two decades—the only remnants of it were the mustard colored waistcoat and violet velvet suit he wore, smudged as they were with dirt. He was but a shadow of himself, and Jacques suspected that it was his guilt that was to blame: guilt for leading Jacques into this helpless and desperate abyss.

But Jacques didn't blame him. He couldn't regret the twenty-one years of life he had just lived, even if it would make their future all the more onerous by contrast. How could he regret meeting Letty or Aunt Emily and coming to know the best parts of them—the best parts of a society so often brimming with contempt and immorality?

And then there was Cecilia. She had been as unexpected as she had been lovable; as maddening as she had been engaging. Did he regret meeting her? Did he regret the gaping hole left in his heart at knowing he would never live the life he had imagined by her side?

Steps sounded with the accompanying jangle of keys.

"Here for us, no doubt," Jacques said, raising himself from the floor.

His father walked over with heavy, shuffling feet as they awaited the opening of the cell door.

"Father," said Jacques, trying to infuse his voice with a confidence he was far from feeling, "don't fret. We will get through this, and we will do it together."

His father looked into his eyes, his own pooling with tears and an unspoken apology.

"You gave me a better life than I could ever have imagined for myself," Jacques said.

His father looked away, jaw clenching. "And now you face a worse life than you could ever have imagined for yourself." He turned his head back to Jacques, with an almost haunted expression. "We will not be looked on with kindness in France."

Jacques suppressed the desire to swallow. Showing the fear he felt would mean adding to the burden of guilt and shame his father already felt.

The jangling of keys stopped, and the door opened with a deafening, drawn-out creak.

The time had come.

21

Cecilia absently stirred her tea with a spoon, watching the way the brown liquid swirled around and around the deep hole in the center where her spoon sat. Her mother spread preserves over her toast, oblivious to Cecilia's inner turmoil.

Cecilia looked up as the door opened to reveal her father, who made his way to the seat at the head of the table, holding a newspaper in his hands.

Averting her eyes, she sipped her tea in silence. Today the Levesques would be tried at the Sessions House. Today they would discover when they would be forced onto a ship to sail across the Channel to the country they hadn't called home in decades.

"Bah!" her father called out suddenly as he spread out the pages of the newspaper. "Quarter Sessions today, and not a moment too soon. Those French paupers have trespassed on our soil for far too long. Our consolation must be that they will be met with anger and hostility even in their own country. I have heard of *émigrés* being beaten and tortured upon their return, and none of *them* impersonated nobility!"

Cecilia swallowed, putting a hand to her stomach, which spun and churned like the tea before her.

"How fortunate we are," said her mother, "that you did not encourage the attentions of such a charlatan! We owe Lord Retsford our loyalty and thanks for exposing the men." She smoothed the napkin on her lap. "I rest easy knowing that you will be well taken care of in the marquess's capable hands, Cecilia."

Cecilia's spoon clanked onto the saucer holding her cup of tea. Her neck, cheeks, and ears felt hot. "I don't believe the marquess has any intention at all of offering for me, Mama. And perhaps that is for the best, as I have no intention at all of accepting him."

Both her parents' hands stilled, her father's newspaper folding over at the top, revealing his perplexed expression.

Her mother laughed nervously. "What ever do you mean, my dear? Of course he means to offer for you. Let us not forget how he singled you out so graciously at his own al fresco party!"

Cecilia shook her head, feeling impatient. "Once he feels that he has my affection, I have no doubt his own attention will shift to another young woman. I understand that Lord Tidwell's daughter will come out next season, and she is generally thought to be the greatest beauty to take the *ton* in years."

She saw dismay fill her mother's eyes, but it was followed by a practical tilting of her head and the resuming of eating. "Then we must take greater pains to ensure he makes an offer before next season begins. I understand he has plans to remove to Brighton next week. I think we may contrive to find ourselves there, too, don't you think, Mr. Cosgrove? A three- or four-week delay in our return to Dorsetshire is surely merited, given the situation." She looked to her husband, who nodded.

"Yes, of course," he said. "But Cecy, my dear, you must exert yourself a little more. Perhaps we need to hire a different maid for you? One who is capable of achieving something a little more flattering than this coiffure you have been wearing of late." He looked with slight distaste at her hair. "And perhaps a little more rouge wouldn't hurt, so long as it is accompanied by your most engaging smile, eh?" He winked at her. "None of this Friday face of yours."

She stood suddenly, the silverware clanking with the jolting of the table. She couldn't bear another second. "I don't *wish* to marry the marquess!" she cried, her chest heaving. Her parents regarded her with blinking, uncomprehending eyes. "And I will not *parade* myself about, stooping to whatever means necessary to ensure his approval—or anyone else's."

Her father's face infused with a pink, then crimson, then purple hue, and he struck his fist on the table. Encountering a warning glance from his wife, he took in a large breath before speaking, managing an unconvincing chuckle. "Now, now, my dear. No one is asking such a thing of you. Besides, what is this? You have always wished to marry just such a man as the marquess! Recall how you convinced me *not* to give my blessing to Lord Brockway when he wished to pay his addresses because you were convinced you could manage a bigger catch."

Cecilia closed her eyes, feeling sick at hearing her own folly repeated back to her. If it hadn't been for Mr. Levesque, she might well still be saying such insufferably proud and arrogant nonsense.

"I was wrong," she said, leaning her hands on the table. "And I am very sorry for the way I have acted in the past. But I simply *cannot* marry someone who I hold in such aversion as I do the marquess. Please understand."

"Well I assure you that I do *not* understand," her father said. "What has aversion to say to marriage? You *will* do this for the Cosgrove name, Cecilia!"

Cecilia glanced at her mother, whose lips were pursed and brows furrowed in thought, and then turned from the room in agitation.

She took the stairs up to her bedroom as quickly as she could, heading straight for her escritoire. She dipped the quill in the ink, ignoring that it needed sharpening. She hardly needed it to look neat, so long as Letty could read it.

She read over it once and blew on the wet ink before folding it and sealing it.

Rushing toward the staircase, she came upon Isabel.

"Good gracious, Cecy," Isabel said, stopping short to prevent a collision. "What has you in such a hurry?"

Cecilia ran her fingers along the folded letter, hesitating for a moment. Isabel could perhaps be a great help. Cecilia could hardly ask her mother to accompany her, but Isabel or Charles could easily do so.

"It is Quarter Sessions today," said Cecilia, almost hoping she wouldn't have to provide more explanation.

"Is it?" Isabel tilted her head to the side, looking at Cecilia with a curious expression. And then her eyes lit up with understanding. "You wish to attend the trial of Lord Moulinet."

Cecilia nodded slowly, looking down at the letter in her hands. "I must see him one more time, if that is all I am allowed. I doubt there is anything I can do to prevent the deportation, but I cannot sit here idly."

Isabel nodded.

"But there is hardly any time," Cecilia said, feeling the rush of impatience pulse through her. "Aunt Emily and Letty plan to attend, I believe, but I am afraid I may have missed my chance to go with them." She looked at Isabel, helpless and pleading.

Isabel scanned her face for a moment and then smiled. "Let me go get Charles." She nodded, indicating the staircase. "You go instruct the chaise to be brought around."

Cecilia grabbed Isabel's hand, swallowing the lump in her throat, grateful that her sister was so willing to be kind despite the unkind treatment Cecilia had subjected her to over the years.

"Go," Isabel said, squeezing Cecilia's hand.

The arrival of Cecilia, Isabel, and Charles at the Middlesex Sessions House coincided with the arrival of various equipages transporting prisoners. Cecilia's heart picked up speed as she watched the prisoners shuffle up the steps of the building, their irons clanking against each other and making loud grating noises on the stairs. They were all filthy, and their stench could be smelt even from twenty feet away.

Would she see Jacques and his father amidst the queue of men—two men she knew didn't belong among such a group of rough criminals?

Charles shook his head with a frown. "I have never been to Newgate, but my visit to Marshalsea was enough for me to see the state in which these men—and women—are kept. They are treated little better than animals."

"I confess," said a voice behind them, "that I did not expect to see you here, Miss Cosgrove." The Marquess of Restford tipped his hat and took another step toward them.

Cecilia felt her hands begin to shake with anger. In her eagerness to see Jacques, she hadn't considered that the marquess might attend. "And I might have guessed that you *would* be here."

He offered a half-smile. "Did I not tell you but a week ago that you had misjudged both me and the vicomte—or Mr. Levesque, rather?"

"You did tell me that," said Cecilia, "but it does not follow that I believe you were correct. Mr. Levesque is still more of a gentleman than you ever will be."

The marquess raised one brow. "I think you will find that the justices of the peace disagree with you."

Cecilia swallowed. "No doubt you have come to ensure that your wishes are carried out."

The marquess inclined his head, and put a hand over his chest. "I have only the wishes of this great country at heart, Miss Cosgrove.

We cannot allow murderers and charlatans to take over—I am certain we all agree upon that at least."

Cecilia blew out a breath through her nose and shook her head, shutting her eyes and trying to remind herself that it would hardly work in Mr. Levesque's favor for her to further antagonize the marquess.

She looked up at him, clasping her hands together. "You don't have to do this, Lord Retsford. Let them be."

Her pleading seemed to anger him, and his jaw hardened. "It is too late." He inclined his head once more, and walked into the building.

Isabel put an arm around Cecilia's shoulders.

"I am afraid," said Charles, looking in the direction of the marquess with narrowed eyes, "that if you marry that man, Miss Cosgrove, you will have to resign yourself to seeing much less of your sister and myself."

"There is no fear of that," Cecilia said softly, watching the last few prisoners trickle into the Sessions House. "I think he became disillusioned with me some time since and has no plans at all to offer anymore."

"Well," Isabel said, "that is surely a mercy, isn't it? Mama and Papa can hardly force you to marry a man who hasn't offered you the option."

Cecilia sighed. "No. But they will never forgive me for inspiring him with a distaste for my company. I think Papa has been engaged in mentally spending the marquess's money and making use of his influence for some time now."

Isabel pulled her more tightly toward her. "Charles and I will do whatever we may to help Mama and Papa see reason, Cecy. You are not alone."

They walked up the stone steps and into the building, coming to the top of a split stone staircase that led down to an entry hall, sun-lit by the rotunda above. Letty and Aunt Emily stood together just beyond the base of one staircase, and it was only a few seconds before Letty caught sight of Cecilia.

Her hand flew to her mouth, and she directed her mother's gaze to the top of the staircases before hurrying across the stone floor and coming up the stairs, her footsteps echoing loudly.

"I knew you loved him! I knew it!" she gushed, embracing Cecilia heartily.

Cecilia returned the embrace, blinking rapidly to dispel the tears in her eyes. What good was her love when she would be watching the first man she ever loved sentenced to deportation? Sent back to a war-torn country where there was nothing for him?

They entered the trial room together as a man in shackles pleaded his case to the three justices sitting before him, flanked by a jury on one side.

"Fourteen years transportation," the chairman declared.

A woman in the audience was heard to break into sobs, and the prisoner was taken away from the room.

Cecilia took her seat between Letty and Aunt Emily, aware that her hands were shaking.

"There he is," Letty said in a hushed voice.

Cecilia's heart jumped, and she followed the direction of Letty's gaze. Jacques sat next to his father, his head hanging down, hair tousled, and streaks of dirt on his cheek. His father, in his conspicuously bright but dirty clothing, stared ahead blankly.

The marquess sat opposite them, his head held high as he nodded his recognition at one of the justices of the peace.

Cecilia's heart sank. There was no hope at all.

Cecilia stared at Jacques, willing him to look at her. Would he be glad to see her there?

He sat up with a large sigh, turning his head to glance at the people in the seats that lined the hall, only to take a second, wide-eyed glance upon seeing Cecilia. His mouth opened slightly, and Cecilia tried to smile at him but had to take her lips between her teeth to keep from crying instead.

She saw a flicker of hope in his eyes, immediately extinguished when it was signaled that it was his turn for trial.

"The case of Misters Hugo and Jacques Levesque, brought to stand trial for violation of the Aliens Act of 1793."

Aunt Emily made a tsking sound. "They had already arrived in England before that act was passed."

Charles shook his head. "It doesn't matter, unfortunately. The Act specifies that foreigners must register with their local justice of the peace, providing their name, rank, address, and occupation. I imagine that they did so with false information, if at all."

"...brought forth by the Most Honorable Marquess of Retsford. How do the accused plead?"

"Not guilty," said Jacques, stepping forward slightly.

He nudged his father, who looked up and said in a barely audible voice, "Not guilty."

Cecilia squeezed her eyes shut, remembering the words of Lady Caroline: "...*the only reason he was discovered was because of* you."

"Your Honor," said Jacques, standing straight, with his shoulders back. "I wish to clarify some particulars about our situation, if I may."

The chairman nodded.

"My father and I came to England's shores nearly twenty-one years ago in the company of the Comte de Montreuil—my father was his valet, and I was somewhat of a pageboy. The Comte feared for his life and safety in France, and so it was that he decided to flee the violence and unfair treatment he believed he would receive at the hands of the French government. He brought over all of the belongings he could—anything of value, as he anticipated a lengthy stay in England.

"While the Comte was not particularly old, he had led a dissolute life, which had left him susceptible to illness and weakness. Unfortunately, the perilous journey to Dover proved too much for him, and he died shortly after our arrival. It was at this point that my father and I had to make some decisions. We had no money to pay for passage back to France, and even if we had, we would likely have been killed upon returning. Alternatively, to send our master's belongings back would be to effectively send them into the hands of the government that had just decided to abolish the existence of the Comte's title—nor did he have any heir that we were aware of. Who had a right to the Comte's valuables, then?

"It was very unclear. We decided that we would use the Comte's belongings to create a life for ourselves in England—the country that had been willing to accept people being pushed from their own country. Since that day, we have done our best to manage and grow the wealth we began with, creating a thriving estate, with happy tenants and successful harvests. If those people were here now, I assure you that they would beg for mercy on our behalf. We stand by our claim that we have been an asset rather than a drain on this beautiful country. We ask for your mercy. Let us stay, Your Honors."

He nodded and took a step back, bringing him back in line with his father, who had silent tears streaming down his face.

Cecilia found that she, too, was crying. Why had she never asked him more about his background, about the life he had lived before meeting her? His deceit had not stemmed, as the marquess had implied, from greed or hunger for power, but simply from a desire to survive. Given the circumstances, what were he and his father to do?

She looked at the two men, standing before the justices and jury, who were all conferring one with another. The glances of two jurymen and one of the justices of the peace were seen to frequently travel to the marquess, who sat gravely, letting his hard eyes travel over them.

"The Lord Retsford," said the chairman, "will please come forward to present his evidence against the accused."

Cecilia's eyes whipped to the marquess, who met hers with a smiling sneer, before nodding at the justice of the peace.

He had no intent whatsoever of saving the Levesques.

❧ 22 ❧

Jacques watched as the marquess made his way away from
them, having made his case against them—a case full of
untruth which could not be proven untrue. His eyes bored into
Jacques with satisfaction and mockery. The marquess would
take them down together, even though he had no quarrel with
Jacques's father.

He had accused them of murdering the Comte, an accusation
which had generated a rumble of murmuring throughout the hall.

It was only one minute—one long, interminable minute—before
the Jury was ready to state their decision.

"The jury," said one of the men, his eyes flitting briefly to the
marquess, "finds the accused guilty."

Jacques's lids closed, and he took in a slow breath.

How had he managed to hope for anything different? It was clear
that the marquess was well-acquainted with at least one of the
justices and multiple members of the jury.

"You are found guilty," the chairman said, as Jacques grasped his
father's shaking hand, "in violation of the Aliens Act of 1793 and are

hereby sentenced to deportation, set to take place in two days' time from the port of Dover, where you will be conveyed..."

The chairman kept speaking, but it sounded muffled in Jacques's ears, as images from the last twenty years flashed through his head.

Arriving at Rothwell Park, tired and terrified, where Aunt Emily had welcomed them, fed them, and cared for them.

Holding baby Letty for the first time, when he had whispered in her ear in French, "I have always wished for a sister."

Playing hide and seek with Letty among the boxwood hedges, where she could never manage to keep her position secret due to her constant giggles.

Stepping into their home at Honiton for the first time, awed at the knowledge that it was theirs.

Tracing the letters of his name on his first calling card.

Rubbing the cloth of his new coat, made of blue superfine.

Meeting Cecilia for the first time, his contempt melting away and morphing into admiration as she danced with Letty on the dark terrace.

The feel of Cecilia's soft lips on his, and the warmth that emanated from the small of her back, where his hand pulled her toward him.

His eyes flew open.

It was all over. It would all be nothing but distant, bittersweet memories in two days.

He felt his father nudge him and looked around. It was time for the next prisoner to face his fate—Jacques could only hope that it would be more kind to him than it had been to them.

A man took hold of Jacques's arm, pulling him away from the bench where the justices sat, white-wigged and unmoved by the plight of the men before them. The chairman began speaking to the prisoner before him—accused of stealing items from the dinner service of his master—and Jacques searched out the faces of Letty, Aunt Emily, and Cecilia.

They were pushing through the benches of attendees, making

their way toward him and his father. Letty was crying freely, Aunt Emily was grave and silent, while Cecilia had her hands tightly clasped in front of her and silent tears trailing down her cheeks.

He swallowed the lump in his throat. What could he possibly say to them? What did one say to such a forgiving family? Or to the woman one loved madly but would never see again?

"Wait," Letty said to the men escorting Jacques and his father. "Please."

Jacques couldn't help but smile sadly as the men obliged, stopping just beyond the doors to the grand hall, in the slanting light of the rotunda. Letty had a way of getting just what she wanted, even from hardened, hefty men like the ones escorting him and his father.

Letty rested one hand on his father's arm and one hand on Jacques's. "Jacques," she said in a tearful voice.

He could see the heartbreak in her eyes and attempted a smile at her. "I will miss you, *ma petite soeur*." He looked to his aunt. "And you, Aunt Emily. You are everything that is good and kind. And I am so sorry."

Aunt Emily covered her mouth and nose with a handkerchief and turned away to hide her emotion.

For the first time since their arrival at the Sessions House, Jacques's father spoke, addressing himself to Letty and Aunt Emily. Jacques gave them their privacy, his heart beat tripping inside as he finally looked to Cecilia.

What did she think of him? Did she believe that he was a murderer? Why had she come? He had seen the hurt and anger in her eyes upon discovering the truth. But today, he had known a glimmer of hope when she had looked at him from the bench inside the hall—hope that she didn't despise him.

He met her eyes, and he watched her mouth tremble as she swallowed, her eyes never wavering from his, even as they filled with more tears.

He shook his head from side to side slowly, wishing he could reach out and take her hand in his, that he could wipe away the tears she could no longer hold in. "I never meant to hurt you or deceive you." He bit his lip to maintain control of his fraying emotions. "I would do anything to make you happy."

She took in a shaky breath, laying a hand to her chest. "I know." She averted her eyes and her head rocked from side to side. "This is all my fault," she said, her voice breaking. She looked up at him, her eyes intent on his. "I love you, Jacques. And I always shall."

Jacques stepped toward her, his hand reaching out impulsively. But the man who held his arm pulled him back firmly, adding his strength to that of the irons, which had already stopped Jacques's movement.

"That's enough, I think," said the man, pulling Jacques forward in an unyielding grip, away from the woman he loved. The woman he would always love.

✤ 23 ✤

Cecilia stared blankly through the chaise window. Isabel and Charles sat across from her, maintaining silence throughout the carriage ride home, respecting Cecilia's grief and somber mood.

She wouldn't give in to tears. Not in the carriage. Not until she could indulge in them as loudly and for as long as she wished, muffling her anger and desperation into her pillow.

How could this be her reality? No sooner had she come to love a man than he was taken from her; no sooner had she given up pretending to be what everyone wanted her to be than the person who had seen her through it all was gone.

She had finally felt real, tangible happiness; hope for the future—until it had evaporated in her grasp without warning.

She was powerless to save the man she wished to spend her life with—the man who had taught her what it meant to open herself to love.

As the carriage rolled to a stop in Belport Street, reckless thoughts passed in and out of her head—sneaking onto the ship that he would board; helping him and his father escape from custody before they could set sail; throwing herself on the mercy of the marquess—offering herself as a sacrifice to save the Levesques.

She thought of Lady Caroline and the way she had smiled contentedly upon Cecilia's admission of her true feelings. Would she be smiling now to know of Jacques's fate?

Lady Caroline had said that Jacques had saved her life three times. Where was she now when Jacques himself needed saving?

Cecilia ran up the stairs, skipping steps at a time, bursting through the door to her bedroom, and pulling a paper toward her as she sat down.

She scrawled a note to Lady Caroline, ignoring the hot tears that dropped onto the page, creating small bubbled bumps as they seeped into the paper.

Folding and sealing it without even taking the time to reread her words, she rang the bell, slipping the note under the door so that she wouldn't be disturbed, and then dropped onto her bed, face in her pillow, until oblivion overtook her.

For the next two days, the hours seemed to creep, while the days themselves slipped by too quickly. The day of the Levesques' deportation arrived, and Cecilia awoke with a gaping hole inside her.

She dressed without speaking more than five words to Anaïs, who, thankfully, seemed sensitive to her mistress's somber mood.

Unwilling to face her parents or the commentary with which they would no doubt fill the silence of the breakfast table, Cecilia asked to take her food upstairs, not venturing from her room all morning.

Even when her breakfast tray was brought in, she found she had no stomach for the tea or toast in front of her.

Her anger toward the marquess and even toward Lady Caroline —from whom she had had not a word—had dulled and numbed, just as the entire world around her seemed to have done. As she sat in front of her mirror, she hardly recognized herself. The sparkling blue of her eyes had been replaced by a dim, flinty hue.

She turned away and walked to the window. Had the Levesques left for Dover already? What would happen to them once they landed at Calais?

She had heard enough stories of *émigrés* returning to their home-land to know that even the best case scenario was hardly reassuring.

A knock sounded, and Cecilia felt a gush of irritation. Could she not have one morning of peace?

"What is it?" she said in a clipped tone.

"It is Lady Caroline Lamb," said Anaïs in her heavy French accent. "She wishes you to ride with her and awaits you outside."

Cecilia's nostrils flared. *Now* she came? Now that it was too late? "Please tell her that I am not at home to visitors."

"Yes, ma'am," said Anaïs, and her footsteps sounded, retreating from the doorway toward the staircase.

Cecilia turned around and leaned her back against the door, resting her head on it. It was hardly fair to take out her frustration on Lady Caroline, and yet her heart wished to place the blame *somewhere*.

A knock sounded again, startling her so that she jumped slightly. It only increased her irritation.

"I do not wish to be disturbed again, Anaïs," she said, trying unsuccessfully to keep the harshness from her voice.

The door pushed open, and she stepped back, eyes wide at the disregard of her orders.

But it was Lady Caroline whose head peeked through the gap, not Anaïs's.

"I hope you will forgive me, Cecilia," she said with a smile, "as you know very well that I do just as I please. And today, it pleases me that you come out riding with me."

Cecilia stared at Lady Caroline, incredulous. How could she be so dead to feeling that she arrived with no forewarning at all, smiling as though Cecilia's world wasn't falling apart before her very eyes?

Seeing that Cecilia had no intention at all of moving, Lady Caroline squeezed into the bedroom, taking the bonnet and gloves Anaïs had left on the table and placing the bonnet squarely onto Cecilia's head.

She looked Cecilia in the eye and put a hand on both of her shoulders. "I know you are hurting. And that is why you must come out with me." She grabbed Cecilia by the hand, pulling her toward the doorway, as if a carriage ride could somehow erase the bleakness of the future Cecilia saw gaping before her, inescapable.

But she hadn't the energy to argue with the bold, flighty woman tugging her into the corridor and then down the stairway.

The bustle of the town streets was oddly calming to Cecilia, as she sat silent, with Lady Caroline beside her, navigating the midday traffic.

Lady Caroline looked over at her intermittently, finally saying, "What a lovely day this is, don't you think?" She glanced up at the sky, where soft clouds inched along with the light breeze.

Cecilia followed suit. At least the weather would be good for the Channel crossing. Cecilia had never crossed over to France, nor did she ever seem likely to be able to, with the neverending war continuing on.

The dome of St. Paul's appeared before them, towering above London. Cecilia hardly knew where Lady Caroline was taking them, nor did she care.

Lady Caroline glanced at her and smiled. "You don't look to be enjoying the ride. I have been told that I am a very skilled driver, you know, but perhaps we would do better to stretch our legs." She slowed the horses, bringing them to a halt in front of St. Paul's Cathedral.

Cecilia sighed. "It has nothing to do with your driving, Lady Caroline."

"And don't I know it?" Lady Caroline replied with a teasing smile.

Cecilia's nostrils flared as she followed Lady Caroline down from the phaeton, using the mounting block below. If Lady Caroline thought that flippancy was the cure for Cecilia's pain, she was terribly wrong.

Lady Caroline linked her arm with Cecilia's, guiding them toward the churchyard. She handed a thick, folded page to Cecilia. "I think you will find this of great interest."

Cecilia frowned and then looked at Lady Caroline. "What is it?"

Lady Caroline wagged her eyebrows. "Only what I have been working on tirelessly for the past few days." She stopped, looking ahead of her with a mischievous smile. "And I think there is someone who would very much like to read it with you."

Cecilia glanced up ahead and froze. Sitting on a bench at the end of the walking path, the solitary person in the churchyard, was Jacques Levesque, hands clasped in his lap. Gone were the irons around his ankles and wrists.

He rose slowly from his seat, his eyes trained on her.

Cecilia's mouth hung open, blinking as though with each closing of her eyes, Jacques might disappear and prove that she was only hallucinating.

But there was no mistaking the dirt marks on his face or the rumpled state of his clothing.

Cecilia turned to Lady Caroline, who smiled gleefully and nodded toward Mr. Levesque. "Go," she said to Cecilia, giving her a push.

It was a push she hardly needed.

Picking up her skirt with the hand that held the folded paper, she rushed toward Jacques, matching his quick pace.

And suddenly, Cecilia stopped, with only a foot between them, both of their chests heaving, his eyes scanning hers with an intensity that made Cecilia's head spin. And then, without a word, he took a last step toward her, taking her cheek in his hand and pulling her mouth to his in a way that made her legs feel feeble.

All of the guilt, the pain, and the dashed hopes of the past week poured into the kiss, searing her lips and her heart until she could hardly bear it.

She pulled back, unable to stand the mystery a moment longer. "How?" she said, immediately wishing to close the distance between them again.

Jacques smiled down at her, the love in his eyes making her feel lightheaded again. "Lady Caroline," he said with a shrug.

They both looked over to where Lady Caroline had been standing, but she was no longer there. She stood at the base of the cathedral with her hands clasped behind her back, looking up at the edifice as if nothing at all out of the ordinary was happening behind her.

"What do you mean?" Cecilia said.

"She arrived just as they were taking us to be transported to Dover. And"— he shrugged again, his eyes as uncomprehending as she felt—"she had a written pardon from the Prince Regent himself."

Cecilia looked over to her friend, utterly awed. She had been so angry at Lady Caroline, feeling abandoned by the woman who shared some responsibility at least in the situation of the man she loved. And all the while, Caro had been working to ensure a happier outcome.

"But Cecilia," he said, sending a thrill through her upon hearing her name on his lips, "I have nothing. No reputation to speak of, no right at all to ask you to marry me." He shook his head. "I..."

"Well," she said, lifting her chin, "you have kissed me twice now, Jacques—once in public"— she made a showy gesture with the hand holding the folded paper, indicating the churchyard around them. "If you refuse to marry me, I am afraid that I will have to sue you for breach of promise."

"What is that?" Jacques asked, indicating the paper in Cecilia's hand.

"I don't know. Lady Caroline only said that we should read it together." She handed it to him, her hands still shaking slightly from the overwhelming emotion of the past few minutes.

He opened the paper, and they stood side by side, staring at it together. Cecilia's hand came up to her mouth as Jacques read the words in a low and quick voice.

In the name and on the behalf of His Majesty. George PR George the third etc. To all to whom these Presents shall come Greeting: Our Will and Pleasure is and We do hereby declare and ordain that from and after the date of this Our Warrant, Jacques Levesque shall be styled, entitled and called, "The Right Honorable Lord Honiton," Baron of Honiton..."

His eyes came up to meet hers, utter disbelief reflected there.

"Letters patent," said Cecilia in awe.

Jacques's hand dropped to his side with the paper, and his eyes sought out Lady Caroline.

She was turned toward them, a grand smile on her face, and she rushed over with quick, light footsteps.

"Good day, Lord Honiton," she said, making a curtsy as she came upon them.

"Lady Caroline," said Cecilia dazedly, "how in the *world* did you manage such a thing?"

She shrugged lightly. "It was only a recounting to Prince George the various times you have come to my aid. And when I informed him that such an act on his part would anger the Marquis of Retsford to no end, it was settled, for he cannot abide the man, you know." She looked to Jacques—or Lord Honiton, rather. "You maintain control of your estate and all the money attached to it—in essence, you are in the same position you were a week ago, except that now you are a Baron"—she inclined her head, a twinkle in her eyes—"for which honor you will obviously have to pay dearly and appear before Parliament."

Cecilia stared at her for a moment and then lunged toward her, wrapping her arms around Lady Caroline's petite figure in a crushing embrace.

Lady Caroline returned it with gusto. "Did I not tell you," she said into Cecilia's ear, "that coming out on a ride with me would do you good?"

Cecilia gave a watery chuckle. "You certainly did."

She pulled away and turned back to Jacques. "What of your father?"

Jacques was still recovering from shock, and he blinked before responding. "He is inside the church, thanking God for our deliverance, of course."

Cecilia smiled. "Well, then. He is likely to be in there still for quite some time once he learns that his son has become a baron during his absence."

Jacques laughed dazedly and then looked at Lady Caroline, his head moving from side to side as if he hadn't the words to match his feelings.

She put up a hand to stop him. "Do not thank me, Lord Honiton. Consider it a step toward evening the scale of my debt to you."

"And now," said Cecilia, nudging him with her elbow, "go give your father the most wonderful surprise of his life."

Jacques looked down at her, his eyes bright and warm, and he took her hand in his. "Only if you come with me."

She nodded, and he stooped down to press his lips to hers one more time—the first in a lifetime of such kisses.

24

Jacques looked around the park with a contented sigh, admiring the tranquility of the scene: leaves rustling lightly above, a cloud-streaked blue sky, and the woman he loved walking beside him, her arm intertwined with his. Mr. and Mrs. Galbraith walked a short distance behind them, granting them their privacy.

The scene was idyllic. And yet he was ready to leave the town. "I think you will like Honiton, my love," he said.

Cecilia glanced up at him with a teasing twinkle in her eye. "More than London? For I have always preferred the town to the country, you know."

"Ah, but then you have never been to Honiton, have you?"

"No, I have not." She smiled, inching closer to him. "Nor have I spent time in the country in the company of *you*."

He made a clucking noise with his tongue and shook his head. "I am afraid that I am even duller in the country than I am in the town. The life you have shown me in town has shocked my sensibilities beyond repair. Prize fights, women dressing up as gentlemen, last-minute pardons"— he shook his head. "It is enough to inspire one with a desire to sit in the library reading for the rest of one's days and never again to venture from home."

Cecilia slapped his arm playfully, and he winked at her.

"But honestly," he said, "what would you say to skipping Brighton altogether and going directly to Honiton?"

"I would say that I have had enough adventure this season to last me a few years at least."

Carriage wheels sounded behind them, and Jacques glanced back in time to see Letty attempting to descend from the carriage before it had even come to a full stop.

"It *is* them, Mama!"

She ran over, and then stopped short, taking on a formal posture and then executing a deep curtsy. "Good morning, the Right Honorable Lord Honiton." She rose from the curtsy with an imperious smile until Jacques kicked at her playfully with a foot.

"Have done, Letty," he said with a suppressed smile. He leaned in toward Cecilia. "Letty refuses to treat me with anything but a smothering degree of formality."

Letty's mischievous smile appeared. "I should not wish to give offense by failing to display due deference—I understand you have powerful allies, my lord."

A nudge in the ribs from Cecilia brought him around to look at her.

"Up ahead," she said.

The Marquess of Retsford was coming upon them, riding on horseback beside a young woman whose fiery red hair peeked from under her bonnet. Lord Retsford's jaw hung slightly open, his nostrils flared, his eyes alight with anger and chagrin.

He slowed his horse, and the woman beside him followed suit.

"Mr. Levesque," he said through clenched teeth and a false smile, "I did not anticipate the need to call for a constable during my ride at the park, and yet, finding you here, I think I must."

"I believe," said Cecilia, in a voice of unalloyed charity, "that you must have meant to address yourself to Lord Honiton?"

Lord Retsford scanned the three of them and then Aunt Emily and the Galbraith's behind, as if he might see a previously unnoticed gentleman.

"This," said Letty, indicating her cousin with a sweeping gesture, "is the Right Honorable Baron of Honiton."

The marquess's eyes moved between them, and he shifted in his saddle, then emitted a forced laugh. "Is this some sort of jest?"

"Not at all," said Cecilia. She turned to Jacques. "What was it? Two days ago when you received the letters patent from Prince George?"

"Yes, I believe your memory serves you correctly, for it was two days ago as well that my father and I were released from Newgate at the Prince Regent's behest."

He looked to the marquess and made a polite bow, forcing his expression into one of politeness to stifle the laugh which threatened to burst through at the confusion written on Lord Retsford's face.

"If you will excuse us, Lord Retsford," said Cecilia with a small curtsy, as she pulled Jacques forward inexorably. Letty offered her own dignified curtsy before following along.

They hadn't gone more than ten steps before Letty covered her mouth, giggling softly. "Oh, I would not have missed that for the world!" She clapped her hands in a gesture of excitement.

"I admit," said Cecilia, "it was *very* satisfying to witness the marquess's confusion—to see him put in his place. And in front of that poor but beautiful soul he seems to now have latched onto."

"*That*," said Letty with authority, "is Lady Rebecca Flinthook, widow of Sir Robin Flinthook, who recently died and left her with more money than she knows what to do with."

"I hope that she captures his fancy," Cecilia said, "and quickly, for that matter." She looked up to Jacques with twinkling eyes. "I am sorry, Lord Honiton, but I don't think anything less than the marquess's marriage to another woman will convince my father to give up on the idea of a match between him and me."

"I, too, hope he marries her," said Letty. "There have been some rumors that Lady Rebecca was connected with her husband's sudden demise, you know. And if that is true, then perhaps she will have enough compassion on society to rid us of her second husband, too!"

Jacques tried to frown at Letty. She wasn't looking at him, though, but rather glancing behind them.

"And now I am afraid that I must go," she said with a sigh, "for I only persuaded Mama to take us through the park in case we might happen upon you here, which I am ever so glad that we did! But she has promised to buy me new trimmings for a bonnet, and I fear that, the longer I make her wait, the fewer she will be willing to purchase."

She hugged Cecilia and then made an exaggerated curtsy to Jacques, running off with a teasing grin tossed over her shoulder before he could kick dirt from the path toward her in retaliation.

Cecilia watched her retreat with a smile and then looked ahead with a scoffing noise.

"Good heavens," she said, "are we to meet the entirety of my family in the park today?"

Tobias was riding toward them, flanked on either side by his friends. He slowed his horse as he came upon them.

"In the park at the fashionable hour, Tobias?" said Cecilia in impressed accents. "How very unlike you."

"Join us," said Jacques. He had the distinct impression that Tobias Cosgrove could do with a change of company—the friends he was often seen among were as likely to get him in trouble with the constable as anything else.

Tobias chuckled. "No, no. Forgive me, Honiton, but the prospect of trailing behind two couples who can see nothing but the person beside them for the fog of love which surrounds them—that is not my idea of an afternoon well spent."

"I should think that the solution to that would be obvious," said Mrs. Galbraith, coming to a stop beside Jacques and Cecilia. "We must find just such a person for *you*." She wagged her eyebrows once at her brother.

Tobias's friends laughed heartily with him. "I think I should prefer the irons you wore a few days ago"—he nodded at Jacques— "to becoming leg shackled. But thank you."

"It is only a matter of time before Papa demands it, Tobias," said Cecilia.

Tobias grinned widely. "Then I shall take the best advantage of whatever time I have left to me."

He and his friends nodded at the four of them and continued on their way.

Jacques watched them ride off, the sound of their laughs carrying behind them.

"I think," said Jacques, "that when your brother falls in love, it will catch him completely off guard and perhaps turn his world upside down." He looked down at Cecilia. "In much the same way that meeting you did to *my* life."

He pulled her closer to him—as close as he could without scandalizing the equipages and fellow pedestrians around them.

"And now that your life has been upturned," Cecilia said, "do you find that you are satisfied with the outcome?"

He looked at her with a half-smile, his heart thumping and his head reeling as he tried to grasp that this was no dream but rather his new reality: the warm eyes looking up at him as though no one existed outside of themselves. *The fog of love*, Tobias had called it.

"I find," he said, coming to a halt and brushing a thumb across her pink cheek, "that when I look back on my life before I knew you existed, I wonder how I didn't expire from the boredom and inanity."

She tilted her head to the side, smiling. "You mean to say that, before you met me, you were never imprisoned?"

He pursed his lips, feigning thought, then shook his head.

"Never competed in a prize fight?"

He shook his head.

"Rescued two women dressed as men?"

He shook his head.

"Made into a peer of the realm by the reigning monarch?"

He put up a finger, narrowing his eyes, but then dropped the finger, shaking his head. "You see what a very dull life I led."

"Well, my lord," she said, "I will endeavor to keep you as entertained in the country as you have been in town."

He reared back, staring at her in mock horror. "That sounds more like a threat than a promise." He narrowed his eyes. "I trust you have not acquired any morbid notions from Letty's tales about the murderous widow Lady Rebecca?"

Cecilia wagged her eyebrows at him. "If I answered you, it would spoil the entertainment entirely."

He threw his head back and laughed heartily.

No, life at Cecilia's side would decidedly not be boring.

EPILOGUE

MONTREUIL, FRANCE 1817

Cecilia stepped down from the carriage onto the dirt road, her gloved hand held within her husband's. He met her eyes with a smile—the smile she could never help but return, even three years later.

She steadied the bonnet on her head and looked to the large iron gate, black and rusted, which stood between them and the row of towering trees lining the drive.

Jacques, too, was looking down the lane, and Cecilia could see the mist of memory which clouded his eyes.

"*Maman! Aide-moi, Maman!*"

Their three-year-old daughter's hand hovered in the air from the door of the carriage.

"*Viens*, Caroline," said Jacques, turning to her and putting out his arms in an invitation for her to jump.

She squatted down with an elated grin and jumped, giggling as he began tickling her immediately.

Cecilia watched with a contented smile, putting a hand to her stomach. It had only started to round.

"Where are we, Papa?" Caroline said, her forehead wrinkled.

Jacques took in a breath and set her down on the ground. "This is where Papa and Grandpapa lived, many years ago."

"And you, too, Mama?"

Cecilia smiled and shook her head. "This is my first time here, too, Caro."

Caroline looked at the gate and up at the trees, then squinted down the lane. "But there is no house."

Jacques chuckled, sharing a glance of enjoyment with Cecilia. "There is! Let me show you."

He nodded at the coachman, and stepped toward the gate, opening it with a creak that made Cecilia clench her teeth and Caroline cover her ears.

"It sounds as though it hasn't been opened in years," Jacques said.

"Perhaps it hasn't," said Cecilia.

Jacques put out his hands, offering one to Cecilia and one to Caroline, and together they walked down the lane to the place where Jacques had spent much of his childhood.

"How does it feel?" Cecilia said as they approached the imposing seat of the Comté de Montreuil. Vines covered most of the facade.

"Very strange," said Jacques in a slow, thoughtful tone.

"Do you wish to leave?" Cecilia said, concerned. She hadn't been sure how her husband would react to seeing the place he had left so long ago, with its memories of an entirely different life.

He turned to her and exhaled, shaking his head and smiling. "No." He squeezed her hand in his, even as Caroline broke away to approach the mysterious house. "I want you to know where I came from."

She pulled him toward her, putting a hand behind his neck and bringing him in for a kiss. "Show me everything."

He stroked her cheek with his thumb, putting his forehead against hers. "I want *her* to know, too. I want her to understand."

Cecilia looked to Caroline, who was pulling the leaves apart to see what lay behind. "Then show *us* everything."

He looked at their daughter with a frown. "I don't want her to be ashamed of where her father came from."

Cecilia smiled at him. "Does she look ashamed?"

His half-smile appeared. Caroline was running toward them, bursting with excitement. "A door, Papa! A door!"

"If you are not ashamed, Jacques," Cecilia said, intertwining her fingers in his, "then she will not be ashamed."

"And you?" he said.

Cecilia brought their clasped hands to her lips and kissed his fingers. "How could I ever be ashamed of the man who taught me how to love? How to live in my own skin?"

She shook her head, looking intently into his eyes. "Show me everything, Jacques."

❧❦❧

J oin my newsletter to keep in touch and learn more about the Regency era! I try to keep it fun and interesting.

You can also connect with me and eight other authors in the Sweet Regency Romance Fans group on Facebook.

If you'd like to read the first chapter of the next book in the series, go ahead and turn the page.

HAZELHURST: A REGENCY ROMANCE
CHAPTER ONE

ASHWORTH PLACE, DORSET, ENGLAND
APRIL 1814

Lady Anne Haywood fiddled with the silver wedding band underneath her white glove, her eyes glazed over as she stared blankly in front of her. Her brows were drawn together, and her dark, wavy hair tied back in a simple bun, just as it had been for days. She had been too anxious to sit for her normal toilette—an elegant coiffure would hardly be set off to advantage by the dark rings under her brown eyes or the gray pallor of her normally porcelain skin. Her dress hung more loosely on her arms and waist, the result of days of hardly eating.

The way she looked, Anthony would hardly recognize his wife if he were to return in this moment.

If he were to return at all.

She shut her eyes. She couldn't think such things. She had to remain hopeful.

Approaching footsteps sounded in the corridor, and she straightened, clasping her hands together and looking toward the door with eyes which darted nervously.

It opened, and her brother, William, Viscount of Ashworth, appeared, hat in his hands and a grim set to his square jaw.

She stood, looking a question at him, and he grimaced, shaking his head with apology written in his eyes and the frowning lines of his face.

Anne took her lips between her teeth and tried to swallow the nausea back down. They hadn't found Anthony.

William stepped toward her and took her hand in his, helping her to sit down on the settee behind her. "I am so very sorry, Anne." He sat down beside her, setting his hat next to him and angling his knees toward her. He kept her hand in his, squeezing it lightly.

"I am afraid I have worse news still."

She tried to take a small, steadying breath, keeping her eyes on her hand. She didn't trust herself to look William in the eye. What worse news could he have?

He took in a breath of his own, and Anne could feel his reluctance in the way he watched her, in the low and slow way he spoke. "The Bow Street Runner was unable to find him, but he *was* able to piece together enough information that a few things have become evident."

Anne closed her eyes, her free hand clutching at her skirts. She hardly knew what to prepare herself for. Her husband had been gone more than three weeks. Disappeared without a word. Was he dead? Is that what William had come to tell her? That she was a widow before she had been married even three months?

"It seems that Anthony Haywood is known by another name."

There was a pause, and Anne's brow furrowed even more deeply. What did he mean? His hesitation didn't bode well, but she couldn't tell what his words implied. She wished he would deliver the news quickly, whatever it was. The suspense was unbearable.

William shifted in his seat. "The Runner traced him to Sussex, using the painting you provided to ask people whether they recognized him. Many did, but all insisted that he was called Nicholas—Nicholas Hackett—and that they hadn't seen him in months. The parish register shows his birth and christening records there."

William set his other hand on top of Anne's, which lay trembling in his hand. "Anne," he said, his voice so gentle that it made her wince in anticipation, "there are records in a parish in London showing that Nicholas Hackett married two years ago."

Anne stilled. Her eyelids fluttered for a moment, and she looked up at William, her lips parting wordlessly as she searched his face. His mouth was drawn into a hard, thin line, his eyes deeply pained.

She shut her eyes and shook her head quickly, disentangling her hands from her brother's and standing.

There had to be another explanation.

William had never taken to Anthony. He had tried more than once to persuade Anne against the match, gently at first and then more firmly as time went on, resulting in the greatest row the siblings had ever had. And though he had apologized and made an effort to act with civility and good nature toward Anthony once Anne had made it clear that they intended to wed, things had been strained with William ever since.

"You never liked him," Anne said, unable to stifle a bit of accusation from her tone. Her arms hung stiffly at her sides, fists clenched.

William sighed. "I shan't deny that. But, Anne, surely you cannot think that I would fabricate such a tale as this? To put you through such misery simply over a matter of personal preference?" He shook his head. "You are my sister, Anne. I love you dearly, and it pains me more than you can imagine to be the bearer of such news."

"It isn't possible," Anne said, turning away from him, her head shaking from side to side slowly. She put a hand to her temple and closed her eyes.

This was only a nightmare. She would awaken shortly to find Anthony beside her, sound asleep, with one arm draped over his forehead and his dark, straight hair mussed, as it always was when he slept.

William let out a gush of air. "I am afraid there isn't room for any doubt, Anne. The Runner spoke with his wife, whom it appears he left in a similar fashion a year or so ago."

Anne swallowed painfully, her hand flying to her mouth to stop the nausea which pulsed through her. *His wife?*

Anne was his wife.

"Her name is Louisa Hackett," William said. "She confirmed that she married Nicholas two years ago."

Anne closed her eyes for a moment and took in a large, shaky breath. She wouldn't go into hysterics, she wouldn't faint in front of William. But with her mind aflutter, she needed to know one thing.

"Do you mean," she said, straightening and looking William in the eye, "that I am not, and never was, married?"

William's mouth drew into another pained grimace. It was answer enough for Anne, but he nodded once, almost imperceptibly, anyway. "Not in the eyes of the law or the church, I fear."

Her throat constricted, and she inclined her head once. "Thank you," she said, managing to keep her voice level. "I should like to be alone now, if you please." She turned away from him, hoping he would take it as a dismissal, since she felt her handle on her emotions fraying with each passing second.

William didn't move, though, and she knew without even looking at him that he was debating with himself over his best course of action.

"Please," she said shakily. "Go."

"As you wish," William said softly.

Anne listened, hearing him rise from the settee and then step toward her, only to pause again and stride out of the room. The door made a small thud as it closed.

She stood, rooted to the spot, her chest rising and falling more rapidly as the seconds passed, her hands trembling. The room swayed in front of her, and she put a hand out to the shelves of books lining the wall to stabilize her. Her nostrils flared and her chin began to tremble before she crumpled into a heap on the floor, bringing two books down with her as she put her head in her hands and cried.

INGLEBURN PARK, DORSET, ENGLAND - JULY 1814

"And all the money gone with him." Lord Purbeck slammed a fist onto the desk in the large library of Ingleburn Park. and Anne winced.

It was not the first time her father had lamented the disappearance of Anne's husband, Anthony.

No, Nicholas. His name was Nicholas Hackett.

She hardly knew how to refer to him anymore. He had never been her husband in a legal sense. She knew that now.

In the two months since William's visit, there had been many such encounters with her father. Anne stood in no doubt of where her father placed the blame for the situation. It would always lie on Anne's shoulders, for she had pleaded with him to countenance the match, had made the case to her father that his fortune more than made up for his lack of title; that it qualified him to marry the daughter of an earl.

And miraculously, her father had relented.

But there had been no fortune. It had all been part of the deception, and Lord Purbeck was unlikely to let Anne forget it for years to come.

"Humiliation such as our family has never known!" Her father's lips were turned down in disgust, and his eyes bored into her as she sat motionless in her chair, waiting for this storm to pass and grant her a reprieve until it built up again in a few days' time.

She did not cower in front of her father, for she was well used to his blustering, and she had her own stubborn streak underneath the complacency she presented. But she kept her eyes trained on the row of books behind him, for she hated the way her father looked when he was in a rage.

He exhaled sharply. "Well," he said in a lighter tone, straightening a paper on his desk, "perhaps we shall come about despite it all."

Anne's eyes whipped over to him. This was not the usual ending to such interviews. But she knew better than to speak.

"I have arranged an advantageous match for you, Anne—a way for you to make amends to this family for the mud you have dragged us through." He stared at her severely, and she clutched her hands together in her lap, willing herself to show a calm she was far from feeling.

The idea of marriage brought on a fresh wave of anxiety—particularly the thought of a match arranged by her father. He wouldn't hesitate for a moment to auction her off to the highest bidder—not with the financial straits the family was in, and not when her own arrangements had ended so disastrously.

Her mind jumped for a moment to the faces of various gentlemen she knew to be widowed or unmarried and possessing significant fortunes. But she brushed away the thought. It hardly mattered. In a moment, her father would reveal the identity of her future husband— her first *real* husband, she thought with a swallow—and she wouldn't fight him on it.

She hadn't the energy. And she knew better than to think such a course would bear any fruit. What would she be arguing for? Another love match?

No. Better to marry someone she disliked than to risk her heart again when it was still reeling from her last marriage—or last attempt at marriage.

"Tobias Cosgrove," her father said, pulling out his snuff box and flicking open the lid carelessly, as though he were revealing something as humdrum as the time.

Anne's brows snapped together.

"Tobias Cosgrove?" she repeated blankly.

He was neither titled nor wealthy, at least to her knowledge. He was merely the son of Mr. and Mrs. Cosgrove, neighbors of Ashworth Place where William and his wife Kate lived.

Her father nodded, looking at her through narrowed eyes. "And very grateful you should be, for it isn't every gentleman would take another man's"—he put a hand up, and Anne felt her cheeks flame. "Well, never mind that," he said. "Suffice it to say that it is a stroke of good fortune I never looked to have. With the success of Cosgrove's most recent investment, they stand in a position to make quite a difference in our fortunes, to say nothing of the advantage of an alliance between the families of Ashworth Place and Hazelhurst."

Anne was only half-listening. She had grown up with Isabel and Cecilia Cosgrove, but her knowledge of their elder brother was limited, off as he had been at school for so much of her life.

The little she *did* know made it hard to believe such a man would agree to marriage at all without significant coercion. His good nature was obvious to anyone who had spent more than a few moments in his company, but it was accompanied by a frivolousness that characterized more than a few determined bachelors of Anne's acquaintance.

She tucked a stray curl behind her ear. At least he would not browbeat her. Indeed, marriage with someone as lighthearted and frivolous as Tobias Cosgrove might be the best she could hope for.

"I trust we are of one accord, Anne," her father said, still watching her with a severity that made her anxious to leave Ingleburn Park and her father's inescapable temper. She could withstand his anger—indeed she would much rather it be directed at her than at her mother—but it wore her down to confront him so often.

She nodded.

"Good," he said, leaning back in his chair and folding his arms. "He will be calling upon you this Thursday. I hope you will show him the civility and gratitude he deserves." He nodded toward the door of the library. "You may go."

She rose from her chair and made a small curtsy to her father, who waved her away with a dismissive hand gesture.

She pulled the door closed gently behind her, knowing how her father's volatile temper could flare up again at something as insignificant as an unexpected noise.

Taking in a deep breath, she walked down the thick carpet of the corridor and up the well-worn stairs. She was coming to dislike her childhood home intensely, riddled as it now was with reminders of her most difficult moments. It had been more difficult than she had anticipated to move home after her marriage had evaporated in an instant, but surely it would not have been easier to stay in the home she had shared with *him*, even if it *did* belong to her.

She had been so terrified of being accidentally referred to or introduced as Lady Anne Haywood that she had avoided social interaction entirely for the last two months. She was Lady Anne Vincent again.

Apparently, though, she would soon be Lady Anne Cosgrove.

She tapped lightly on the door of the parlor which adjoined her mother's room. Her mother had been her saving grace through everything that had happened—a calm, sympathetic presence; someone who was familiar with heartache and unmet expectations.

Anne opened the door enough to peek her head into the room. Her mother sat in the wingback chair, a book open in her hands as she looked to Anne with the warm smile she reserved for her children. Her face was lined—a mixture of smile lines around her eyes and the sorrowful lines on her forehead that almost three decades of marriage to an authoritarian husband had chiseled there.

"Come in, my dear," she said, extending a hand to welcome her.

The weight of the interaction with her father melted at the sight of her mother's kind smile, and she sat on the floor in front of her, just as she had often done as a child, when her mother would run her fingers through Anne's hair and sing to her.

Anne breathed in her mother's violet scent and rested her head on her mother's knee. "Did Father tell you?" she asked.

"Tell me what, my dear?"

Anne sighed deeply, letting her shoulders relax even further to counteract the anxiety that crept in at the thought of the future. "I am to be married."

Her mother's hand stopped, her fingertips resting against the crown of Anne's head.

"To Tobias Cosgrove," Anne said.

There was a pause before her mother's hand dropped to Anne's shoulder. "No, he did not tell me."

Anne might have guessed. Her father never *did* tell her mother anything. Whether that was the result of his unapologetic disinterest or the result of the distance her mother kept from him, Anne wasn't sure.

"I cannot claim to know Tobias Cosgrove very well," her mother said, stroking her hair once again, "or precisely what type of husband he might be, but I do think him far preferable to the man I feared your father might choose."

Lord Granworth. Anne suppressed a shudder. Yes, Tobias Cosgrove was decidedly better than Lord Granworth whose squat but self-assured strut and the disquieting way he raked his hungry eyes over every woman sent a shudder through Anne.

"Yes," Anne said on a sigh, "I should be grateful, I'm sure."

Her mother placed her hands upon Anne's shoulders, turning her toward her. "You have known more than your fair share of pain, Anne. Perhaps Tobias Cosgrove is precisely the type of husband you need—one to help you remember the joys of life and how to laugh away your sorrow." She touched a hand to the small curl that hung in front of Anne's ear, too short to reach to her bun. "And who knows but what you might come to care for one another deeply in time?"

Anne turned away, a catch in her throat and a burning in her eyes. "I don't wish for that, Mama." She shut her eyes and inhaled. "I only want to live in peace—neither adored nor despised, neither adoring nor despising."

Her mother kissed the crown of her head. "It is no wonder, my dear, if that is so. Your heart has hardly had time to heal."

Anne said nothing. It wasn't time which was lacking. She had embraced her love match, so desperate that her own marriage not echo her parents' that she had fallen headlong into heartbreak of another kind; so desperate that she had fallen for someone who never even existed.

She would not do it again. She would marry Tobias Cosgrove, and they would have, she hoped, the mutually indifferent marriage of convenience that would give her the peace and independence she needed.

C ontinue reading *Hazelhurst* on Amazon or Kindle Unlimited.

OTHER TITLES BY MARTHA KEYES

If you enjoyed this book, make sure to check out my other books:

Families of Dorset Series

Wyndcross: A Regency Romance (Book One)

Isabel: A Regency Romance (Book Two)

Cecilia: A Regency Romance (Book Three)

Hazelhurst: A Regency Romance (Book Four)

Phoebe: A Regency Romance (Series Novelette)

Regency Shakespeare Series

A Foolish Heart (Book One)

My Wild Heart (Book Two)

True of Heart (Book Three)

Other Titles

Of Lands High and Low

The Christmas Foundling (Belles of Christmas: Frost Fair Book Five)

Goodwill for the Gentleman (Belles of Christmas Book Two)

Eleanor: A Regency Romance

The Road through Rushbury (Seasons of Change Book One)

Join my Newsletter to keep in touch and learn more about the Regency era!
I try to keep it fun and interesting.

OR follow me on BookBub to see my recommendations and get alerts about
my new releases.

AUTHOR'S NOTE

In *Cecilia: A Regency Romance*, you encountered a character named Lady Caroline Lamb. Lady Caroline is a historical figure who lived during the Regency era. She was a bit of a celebrity at the time, hailing as she did from a powerful family (she grew up in Devonshire House) and causing a great deal of scandal, largely connected to her affair with the famous poet Lord Byron. I have taken the liberty of incorporating her into this story, pulling general bits and pieces from her life and weaving them into the storyline.

Lady Caroline was eccentric, and she was known to dress as a man at times, shocking both her husband (who became Prime Minister after Lady Caroline's unfortunate demise) and society as a whole. Her short but intense affair with Lord Byron was public knowledge, and its collapse greatly affected her for years. The scene in *Cecilia* at Lady Heathcote's ball is based off of true events, gruesome as it may seem to readers. I hope I have managed to convey a bit of the complexity in Lady Caroline, even though she is a side character.

As always, I strive to be true to the time period by my research, but I am by no means perfect. I apologize if you encounter errors in *Cecilia*, and I hope that you enjoy the characters and the story.

Thank you for reading *Cecilia*.

Martha Keyes

ABOUT THE AUTHOR

Martha Keyes was born, raised, and educated in Utah—a home she loves dearly but also dearly loves to escape whenever she can travel the world. She received a BA in French Studies and a Master of Public Health, both from Brigham Young University.

Word crafting has always fascinated and motivated her, but it wasn't until a few years ago that she considered writing her own stories. When she isn't writing, she is honing her photography skills, looking for travel deals, and spending time with her husband and children. She lives with her husband and twin boys in Vineyard, Utah.

ACKNOWLEDGMENTS

There are always a few key people who are instrumental in the creation of a novel. My mom has rooted for me and my characters from the very beginning and given me valuable feedback. My dad has encouraged me on some of my worst days, providing a buoying influence during the ups and downs of the writing and publishing process.

My husband has given up precious work hours of his own in order for me to write, edit, write, edit, *ad nauseum*. My little boys are almost always good sports about their scatterbrained mom and my constant sneaking away to the computer to get down an idea while it's fresh.

Thank you to my editor, Jenny Proctor, for her wonderful feedback—I'm so glad I have you!

Thank you to my Review Team for your help and support in an often nerve-wracking business.

And as always, thank you to all my fellow Regency authors and to the wonderful communities of The Writing Gals and LDS Beta Readers. I would be lost without all of your help and trailblazing!

Printed in Great Britain
by Amazon

14698514R00123